AS **EASY** AS **FALLING**
OFF THE FACE OF THE
# EARTH

# LYNNE RAE
# PERKINS

Winner of the Newbery Medal for *Criss Cross*

# AS EASY AS FALLING
## OFF THE FACE OF THE
# EARTH

## Greenwillow Books
*An Imprint of HarperCollinsPublishers*

Thank you to Bill, Lucy, and Frank for various and sundry (but crucial!) bits of information, plot assistance, moral support, and frequently, dinner. Thanks to Frank, especially, for accompanying me to Montana at the drop of a hat. Thank you, Tom K., for sailboat guidance. Thank you, Paul K., for building a homemade airplane. Thank you, Candace N., Eli S., and their friend Lilly for Spanish translation. Thank you to everyone at Greenwillow Books, for everything.

As Easy as Falling Off the Face of the Earth
Copyright © 2010 by Lynne Rae Perkins
First published in 2010 in hardcover; first paperback edition, 2012.

The text of this book is set in Candida BT.
Book design by Sylvie Le Floc'h

Library of Congress Cataloging-in-Publication Data

Perkins, Lynne Rae.
As easy as falling off the face of the earth / Lynne Rae Perkins.
p. cm.
"Greenwillow Books."
Summary: A teenaged boy encounters one comedic calamity after another when his train strands him in the middle of nowhere, and everything comes down to luck.
ISBN 978-0-06-187090-3 (trade bdg.) — ISBN 978-0-06-187091-0 (lib. bdg.)
ISBN 978-0-06-187092-7 (pbk.)
[1. Adventure and adventurers—Fiction. 2. Accidents—Fiction.
3. Luck—Fiction.] I. Title.
PZ7.P4313As 2010 [Fic]—dc22 2009042524

12 13 14 15 16 CG/RRDH 10 9 8 7 6 5 4 3 2 1

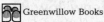 Greenwillow Books

*for a friend*

# CONTENTS

## Part One

## Part Two

## Part Three

## Part Four

# AS EASY AS FALLING OFF THE FACE OF THE EARTH

# PART ONE

# WAIT

Wait a minute.

Was the—had the train just moved?

Ry turned his head to look at it straight on, but it sat on the tracks, as still as the lumpy brown hill he was climbing. As still as the grass that baked in gentle swells as far as he could see and the air in the empty blue sky.

He must have imagined it. Nothing had moved. Everything was the same.

But there it was again. Was it because he blinked? Maybe it was the water in his eyes; it had wobbled up his vision.

He picked out a post alongside the tracks, directly below the line where the logo on the train changed from red to blue. As he watched, the red and the blue shifted almost imperceptibly to the right above the post. Then perceptibly. The train was moving.

"Wait," Ry said aloud.

Because it wasn't supposed to move yet. The conductor had said—the conductor had said forty minutes. Ry was supposed to be on the train. After a full second of hesitation, he went scrambling down the steep rubbled face of the hill. He was thinking that there was time, that trains usually moved a little, in fits and starts, before they really got going. Probably he would get back on the train and then sit there waiting for another hour. But he was thinking it would be smarter to run than to watch it leave without him.

He was leaping and skidding, and he had just glanced up to check on the train when his right foot came down at the wrong angle on a surprise outcropping. He went tumbling in an out-of-control (but time-saving) way down to the scrubby thickets on the lower half of the slope.

Abraded and gravel encrusted, he rose in an instant to his feet. His boots had filled with pebbles and dirt. It felt as if beanbags were strapped to the bottoms of his feet as he thrashed through branchy turnstiles of brush in as straight a line as he could manage.

On his way up the hill, he had picked out a winding

path through the wider spaces, but there wasn't time for that now. He no longer had to blink to see that the train was moving. It was passing before his eyes. People visible in the windows read their magazines, leaned back, lifted cups or cans to take a drink. His heart seemed to have moved inside of his windpipe. He willed it back down into his chest so he could keep breathing.

A small child saw him and waved. Ry waved, too, and shouted. His shout was lost in the roar of the train, but the boy beamed, delighted, before he turned away and was carried out of sight.

When Ry came to the barbed-wire fence, keeping who-knows-what in or out, he slowed himself to pay attention, to avoid snagging cloth or flesh. Still, he was over it in a flash, and running.

No one stood watching from the back of the caboose as he reached the clearing. There was no caboose. The sound of the train faded, and he could hear his own deep gulps for air. He felt his heart thumping along.

The train melted from a recognizable object to a guessable shape to a black dot identifiable only by its position at the vanishing point of a set of railroad tracks. Ry watched the black dot until he could not see it at all. Though he breathed evenly now, and his heart was beating at its usual rhythm, it wasn't because he was calm. It was just that his body hadn't yet heard from his brain that they were in dire straits. Because his brain was still puzzling it out.

For many, many minutes he looked, unbelieving, at the empty air where the train had been. Then he turned in the other direction. It was a mirror image of emptiness, with an identical lesson in perspective. From either side of the tracks, more emptiness extended. There was the north emptiness, made of the strange eroded hills, and the south emptiness, with the grass and, in the distance, a blue-gray shape that must have been a butte.

The south emptiness had a shallow silty river, fringed sparsely with a few trees and bushes, flowing in rough parallel to the tracks. As his brain began to take in what had just happened, Ry's body walked over to one of the trees and sat down on a small boulder in its spotty shade. He untied his hiking boots, pulled them off, and held them upside down. The gravel and dirt spilled out like sands through the hourglass onto the geological time heap of wherever this was.

It felt good to have his shoes off. Ry pulled his socks off, too, and scooted himself around to where he could get his feet in the water. This was so nice that for half a minute, he forgot how he came to be sitting there. Then he remembered, and said some words. There was one word in particular that he said over and over and over. He said it until it didn't even sound like a word anymore. Until he felt almost calm. Then he said to himself, "It's not the end of the world," and that was true. It wasn't the end of the world at all. It might, though, be the middle of nowhere.

His backpack was traveling west in the overhead compartment of the air-conditioned train. No one would miss him for a while, or maybe ever; he had been careful about that. Now he looked at his watch again. Time was so weird. Exactly and only one hour had passed since he had opened that letter.

He had received the letter, with the yellow new-address forwarding sticker and "Urgent—important information" stamped on the envelope in red ink, several days ago. But it was like *Peter and the Wolf*, no, wait— it was like "The Boy Who Cried Wolf." The letters with "Urgent—important information" stamped in red had been arriving regularly from the camp director, and at first Ry would tear them open immediately. Inside, there would be a photocopied note reminding him to bring

Gold Bond powder to prevent chafing, or to wear his boots for an hour every day to break them in, to study up on this or that epoch, or that the itinerary had been altered slightly due to unforeseen circumstances but don't worry, it would still be great.

The last one he had opened before this one had been kind of weird, he remembered that now, but to tell the truth, he hadn't read it that carefully. There was so much going on; the moving truck bringing the furniture, his grandfather arriving, his parents leaving for their trip. He tried to remember now what it had said. Because this one said only—he took it out of his pocket to read it one more time:

Dear Roy,

*Do not come to camp. There is no camp. Camp is a concept that no longer exists in a real place or time.*

We are so sorry. The Summer ArchaeoTrails Program will not take place. A statistically improbable number of things have gone wrong and the camel's back is broken. Your money will be fully refunded as soon as I sell my car and remortgage my house.

We apologize for any inconvenience this may cause, blahblahblah. We hope to regroup and put together a bombproof program by next summer. Live and learn!

    With deepest apologies, believe me,

    (illegible scrawl)

    Wally Osfeld

He almost hadn't opened it at all. He had come across it by accident, standing in the aisle reaching up into the overhead compartment, trying to search through his backpack without actually taking it down out of the bin, looking in all the zipper pouches for the bag of Peanut M&M's. He saw the envelope and thought, I guess I better see what this one says. He sat down, opened it, read it, thought, What the . . . ?

Montana rolled by outside his window as he read it again.

He pulled out his cell phone to call his grandfather, but there were zero bars of reception. The battery was running down, too. Ry wished he hadn't texted his way across Wisconsin and Minnesota, friends from his former life, in his old hometown. He had tried to charge it in the outlet in the restroom, but the outlet was worn out or something; the charger just fell out. Plus it would be not only rude but smelly to sit there for the amount of time it would take. So he hadn't.

7

Just then the train slowed to a crawl. And slowed some more, to a creep. And then it stopped altogether. Ry couldn't see a station, or a town. Or anything, really.

After a few minutes, a conductor appeared and announced that there would be a delay. A minor mechanical problem.

"Do not get off the train," he said. "The train will move on as soon as the problem is resolved. Which will not be long."

But he told the elderly woman in front of Ry, in a lowered voice, that it would be forty minutes or so before the train moved on. An hour at most, he said. And he moved back through the doors to the next car to spread the news.

Ry sat there with his phone in his hand and the letter in his lap.

He just needed to talk to his grandfather.

Probably the train itself (being inside of it) was blocking reception. He would just step off for two minutes, make the call, get back inside. He slipped down the narrow, turning stairwell to the vestibule. No one was there. There were two handles on the door. But would moving them set off some kind of alarm? He had one hand tentatively on the handle when a voice behind him said, "You wanna go out?" Ry turned to see the lady in the red baseball shirt, the one who had slept with a practically life-sized teddy bear.

"I was just going to try to make a phone call," he said.

"Whatever," she said. "I open 'em when I need to step out for a smoke. Here: you just—"

She moved the handles and the door was open.

"I wouldn't go too far, though," she said, and disappeared into one of the restrooms.

Ha! Victory!

But standing outside the train, there was still no signal.

And a few feet away, no signal.

The hills were not that far off, really. Ry had a feeling that up on top of them, he could get enough reception. He checked his watch. If he was not at the top in ten minutes, he would turn around and come back. It crossed his mind that someone looking from the train might see him go, but he decided not to worry about it. He would just act like he knew what he was doing.

As if he knew what he was doing, he strode through the scrubby grass. Casually, but also carefully, he climbed over a barbed-wire fence. Fortunately, it was not an electrified fence, at least at that juncture. The hills, when he reached them, were higher and steeper than he had imagined they would be. By going around behind the one in front, he found a more manageable ascent. Still, it was tricky. But fun.

He was having a good time hauling himself up and along. What a great summer it was going to be. Then remembering, and it was, Oh. Yeah.

He headed for a small flat area on a shoulder of rock. It wasn't the top, but it was probably close enough. The shoulder was tiny enough when he got there that it was a challenge to turn from his knees to a sitting position. Once he had managed that, it was like sitting on any other pinnacle on Earth, which is to say, it was kind of spectacular.

There was what might be a town in the far distance, and the train, not toylike, but smaller than up close. But you could ignore the train and the town, and then it just seemed like the land went on uninterrupted forever, in lumps and bumps of one kind or another. Someone had told him there was a county in Montana that had only one resident. He didn't know if that was true, but if it was, it looked like this could be the one. A pretty little river meandered along below, on the other side of the tracks. The sky, as promised, was Big.

He was balanced between all of it, precariously enough for a thrill, but short of actual danger. He glanced back down at the train. They were missing it all, sitting there with their magazines, eating nachos, only seeing the world through a window.

That was when the train had moved.

And after he was sure it had moved, that was when he gave himself over to gravity.

But too late.

Now, sitting under the tree, he looked back up at where he had climbed and thought two potentially useful thoughts. One was about that town he had seen in the distance. The other was that he hadn't actually had a chance, while he was up there, to try to make the phone call.

He decided to go back up.

The second climbing felt oddly familiar. Like, Oh, yeah, there's that rock. There's that bush. That skidded-out place was made by my own tumbling body.

It was possible that no human had ever climbed this hill before, that he was the only one. Maybe someone prehistoric had climbed it. Or one of the guys laying the track for the railroad, way back when. Why else would anyone be here?

As he climbed, the sound of a rusty hinge creaking open and shut emanated from Ry's stomach and he realized he hadn't eaten for a while, and that he would enjoy eating something about now. That wasn't going to happen right away, so he blocked the thought out. He wasn't going to starve. Yet. He didn't think.

He made his way once more to the place where he had sat the first time, and once more performed the maneuver by which he could turn and sit without falling off. The desolate brown hills still crouched there like ghosts carved out of solid time. The ceiling of sky was an optical illusion made by the atmosphere sucking up all of the colors of sunlight except blue—was that it? When it was just space going on from here to forever, really, with a flimsy veil of gases and moisture in between. The rolling grasslands rolled on and on.

Although he could see the town in the distance. Just barely, but he could see it. This time up, Ry didn't ignore it. He sought it out. It was far away, but it couldn't be that far if he could see it. He could walk there, if he could see it.

Reassured, he pulled his phone out of his pocket.

# IT SEEMED TO RY AT THIS MOMENT THAT HAVING A CELL PHONE IN MONTANA WAS LIKE HAVING A CANOE ON MARS

There was one bar of reception.

Ry called his own house first, where his grandfather was staying, along with the dogs. It was nice to hear another voice, even if it was his own, on the answering machine. He listened, then left a message that he hoped sounded urgent ("Something unexpected has come up and I need to talk to you to figure out what to do about it"), without sounding too alarming ("Don't worry, I'm okay"). His grandfather was an old guy. He didn't want to make him panic.

Wondering if his grandfather would remember to check the answering machine, he called his parents' cell phone. Another thing he didn't want to do was to wreck their Caribbean Sailing Idyll, but this seemed like a circumstance they would want to know about.

"Come on, you guys, answer your phone," he said as it rang and rang.

What was left of the battery was fading from searching so hard for the faint signal, so he turned the phone off. It sang out its good-bye and turned out the lights.

"Okay," he said aloud.

He looked again at the town. He would walk. He would walk along the train tracks. The tracks probably went through the town, or near it. The river was nearby, at least here, so he could take drinks. There would be people in the town, and he would figure out what to do next.

Unless it's a ghost town, he thought, which almost made him laugh. But not quite. He was in the West. That could happen here.

# WALKING
# TO
# TOWN

It was not long before Ry felt that the sun and dry air might be baking his brain. He thought he could feel it begin to shrivel and misfire, maybe even vitrify, inside his skull. But when he walked over to the river and waded in and splashed his face and stood in the shade for five minutes, his brain seemed to reconstitute and he could go on.

He came to a place where a road crossed the tracks, and he had to think, Road or tracks? Road or tracks? Tracks won because they looked straighter. Very, very straight.

On one of his forays into the river, something brushed against his leg as he stood there. He looked down to see a number of fish, each one about the size of his forearm, all swimming along. He didn't know what kind they were. He fingered the pocketknife in his pocket and mentally pictured himself sharpening the end of a stick and trying to spear one of the fish. He could picture sharpening the stick, but in his mind's eye every time he took a stab, he either missed or just knocked the fish off course. How long would it take you, what was the learning curve on fish stabbing? Maybe he should give it a try while he still had strength. Then there would be the whole starting-a-fire-with-a-stick thing. Unless he ate the fish raw.

"I think you can go for pretty long without eating," he said aloud. "As long as you have water to drink."

He sat on the bank, putting his boots back on, and a white shape in the weeds caught his eye. He picked it up. It was the skull of a small animal. He laughed softly as a thought struck him. The thought was that he had expected to spend his summer hiking and looking for bones. He had wanted to do it because it seemed like it would be doing something real. And here he was, hiking, and here was a skull. And it all felt pretty real, right?

The difference was that instead of hiking with a small group of people and a guide who knew where to go, he was utterly alone and not one person in the entire world knew exactly where he was, including himself. And he hadn't expected his hike to be along a railroad track.

But although the track didn't make for the most interesting hike, it was not interestingness he needed most. He just needed to get somewhere.

Ry turned the skull over and looked at it from various angles. What was it? Looking into its vacant eye sockets he said, "You were probably a large rodent. I'm guessing not that long ago."

He held it in one hand as he got to his feet, then slipped it into a side pocket of his shorts. He would find out later what it was. It might be cool to put it on his dresser at home. The truth was that it made him feel a little less alone.

He took inventory of what else was in his pockets. It was a short list: pocketknife, next-to-useless cell phone, wallet. The list of what he didn't have at the moment was longer.

"But at least I have my health," he said. It was a joke.

The wallet had eighty-three dollars in it, a hundred bucks less the cost of some Amtrak food. He looked around for a place to spend it. "Where's the 7-eleven?" he asked. This was a joke, too.

He said his lame jokes aloud, to keep his spirits up. He didn't know if he should panic or not. Well—he knew he shouldn't panic. But he didn't know how dire his situation was. It was the moment when the elevator drops and you don't know whether to laugh or get started on the screening of your whole life passing before your eyes. Only a lot longer than that moment. It was that moment stretched into hours.

Periodically, he felt the urge to text someone.

*Nowhere*, he imagined typing.

*Still nowhere.*

Each time, without thinking, he pulled out his phone, looked at its blank face, remembered, and shoved it back down in his pocket.

"It's not like I'm the only living thing, though," he said. "Look. Cows." Black ones grazed on a hilltop in the distance.

It was probably a great place to be a cow. Or a pheasant. One of which fluttered up from the grasses at his approach.

He walked past a field where cylindrical bales of hay were sprinkled like giant corks spilled on a tabletop. A dilapidated long-ago schoolhouse. A conglomeration of rusted buildings. A cluster of newer silvery ones. Ry stared for a long time at a small house painted bright orange with about twenty cars parked behind it, in varying states of decay, along with discarded bathroom fixtures and a windowless bus that seemed to have melted into the ground, faded to an almost greenish yellow, vegetation thriving around it and up through it. He decided to keep walking toward the little town.

Down here in the bottomlands, Ry couldn't see it. It had to be just beyond those next hills, though. Should he use his energy to climb up high again? What if night fell before he got there? No. It couldn't be that far. How often did trains come along, and would a train stop and pick up someone waving their arms? He didn't think so. Would a train stop if the engineer saw a dead body near the tracks? Maybe the engineer would tell someone. But maybe he would be looking the other way.

The track split into two tracks now. That could be a good sign.

His stomach made the sound effect for a cartoon character hurtling through outer space in a spiral trajectory. The bones in his legs were softening into rubber bands. His forearms were covered with tiny scratches that were more painful than they looked.

Ry felt a sudden trickling from his nose, and then a flowing. He turned his head and lifted his arm to wipe it on the sleeve of his T-shirt and saw that it was blood. His nose was bleeding. Lifting the hem of his T-shirt and pinching his nose shut with it, he plodded along, breathing through his mouth, checking every few minutes to see if the bleeding had stopped.

The sun was beginning to lower in the sky, shifting its strategy from beating down on his head and shoulders to blinding him. Ry started over to the river again and, without intending to, found himself sitting down halfway there. He

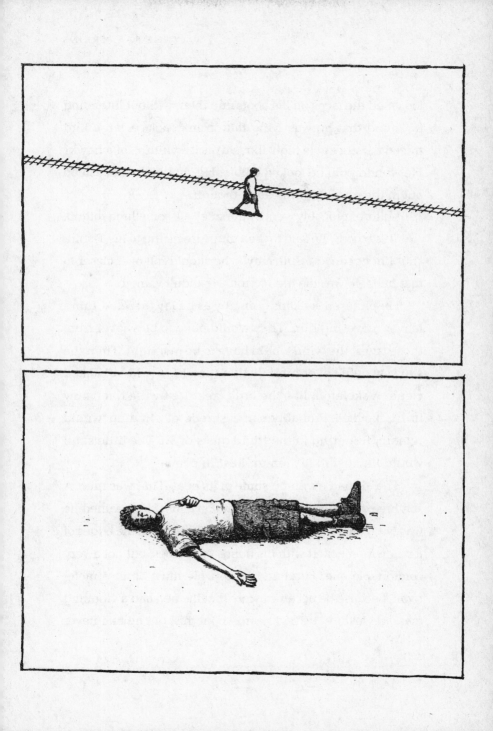

loosened the laces on his boots and then, without intending to, found that he was lying flat on his back. A large bird traced a silent circle high above. Was it a vulture, or a hawk? He wondered if he looked edible. He should not fall asleep out in the open. He was tired, though.

Vultures probably went by the smell. Of something rotting.

"It's blood," he said to the vulture, referring to his T-shirt, "but I'm not dead." Still, maybe he should roll over closer to that tree. He was too tired to roll. He didn't want to.

He pictured seasons going by as he lay there. Autumn leaves, covering him. They would have to blow over from those trees; the wind would have to be just right. Then the snows would cover him. By that time he would be picked clean. A skeleton, like the little creature by the river, now in his pocket. Probably some shreds of clothing would remain, fluttering in the frigid gusts of air. The little skull would lie next to his femur. Rest in peace.

The air had given up some of its heat. That was nice. A soft breeze floated over Ry's closed eyelids. He dreamed he was lying on a bed. A huge bed; he couldn't find the edges of it when he reached with his hands or his toes, but not a very comfortable one. Hard and lumpy. He must be in a motel room, because he became aware that the bed had a vibrating massage feature. Ry had heard about this, but he had never seen one before. There was a metal box with a slot to put quarters in, to make it go. He was surprised at how loud it was, though—the loudness was canceling out most of the relaxingness. There was also a jerkiness to it, a stop-and-start irregularness, like trying to sleep when your neighbor was cutting up logs with a chain saw. He examined the metal box to see if he could adjust the setting, turn it down, but there were no knobs or dials, just the slot for quarters.

Then he sat up and opened his eyes.

A freight train was rolling by. It seemed to be slowing down; the sound of the steel wheels reached him in gently lurching waves as one by one the boxcars and tankers flowed along before him.

Ry thought he saw two figures, moving shadows, through the open door of a boxcar, and he saw that here was an opportunity for rescue. A way to shortcut his long hike. But the silhouettes gave him the creeps, too. And besides, most of the boxcar doors were shut.

He was on his feet now. He watched uncertainly for a time. The train seemed to be going slower and slower, slowing down to a complete. Stop.

Directly before him, a short set of metal steps led up to a metal mesh door in the metal mesh walls of a car carrier. If they hadn't stopped so directly before him, beckoning him, he probably wouldn't have climbed on. But there they were. As if under a spell, he walked to them and hauled himself up. He climbed to the top step and tried the door. It was locked, so he turned around and sat down.

A few minutes later, there was a growing rumbling. When Ry stood up and leaned around, he could see between his car and the next that another train was passing in the opposite direction, on the second track.

Not long after the rumbling faded, his train began to move again. Slowly at first. Then continuing slowly. And slowly some more. The train never did move faster than very slowly while Ry was on it, because it was making its way onto a siding in a freight yard on the outskirts of the town. He had hopped onto the train just a mile or so out. He could have walked it, though he didn't know that when he got on. He couldn't see the town at the beginning of the track's long, gradual curve. Even when he could see it, he was glad to be riding.

He rode with his legs stretched out, the backs of his heels resting against a lower step, watching this chunk of the world scroll by. When the train went over the river, on the trestle, Ry pulled his legs and feet up instinctively, uninstinctively forgetting how he had loosened his bootlaces earlier. His left boot caught on the edge of the metal step, his foot slipped out of the boot, and the boot bounced once on the trestle and went sailing through the air, down into the milky coffee of the river water. He saw it reemerge to bob along downstream like a plastic duck in a carnival booth, way, way, way out of reach. He watched it in disbelief, his boot floating off to end up in some distant weedy backwater or at the bottom of the river, not doing anyone any good, while here was his foot in only a sock, his foot that the boot fit perfectly, never again to meet. He pulled the laces tight on the remaining boot and tied them.

The train slowed further as it pulled past—humans! Sitting in lawn chairs, next to a little house. Concrete grain elevators. A scrapyard full of heaps of curled metal rubbish. And the trainyard. Suddenly there were several tracks, and other trains, and pieces of trains, unidentified industrial objects, buildings. And people working.

Ry decided to jump off before they saw him sitting there. The train was barely moving. He jumped without incident and limped (on account of the missing boot) hurriedly over behind some rusting piles of industrial detritus. Not seeing an inch-thick rusted steel cable because it was in shadow and coming straight at him, he walked into it. It hit him just above his right eye. He jumped back and let out a yelp and his hand flew up

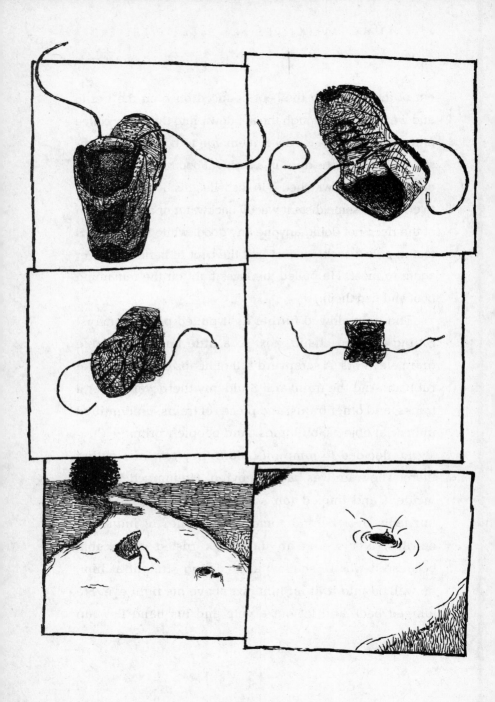

to where the pain was. He clenched his eye shut and hopped up and down in a circle.

Then he stood still. He moved his hand up just slightly and opened his eye.

"I can still see," he said. "That's good." He took his hand away and looked at it.

"No blood," he said. "That's lucky."

He couldn't help smiling a little despite the searing pain, because this made him think of the joke about the blind dog with three legs, no tail, and major bald patches.

"What's his name?" someone asks.

"Lucky," says the dog's owner.

He stood there on the rusted, frayed edge of some town in Montana at sunset. He could feel warmth around his eye as the swelling narrowed his eye opening to a slit. But it didn't swell shut completely. That was lucky.

"I'm so lucky," he said to himself. "Lucky, lucky, lucky."

Ry had been happy to see the town on the horizon, but now that he was here, what was he supposed to do? Where should he go? Who should he talk to? He pulled out his phone again and turned it on. There were five messages:

Jake was bored—how was the train? Amanda just saw that one guy at the mall. Again. From Eric: *Dude, you at camp yet?* From Nina: *Hey, have you talked to Amanda? She won't talk to me.* From Connor: *Wanna play b-ball?*

"I don't live there anymore, remember?" muttered Ry.

He sent out a mass text: *Where am I??!!??*

No Grandpa, no parents yet. He called them both.

"Call me," he said. "I have to turn my phone off, but leave a message."

Food, he thought then. I have to eat.

He did have some money in his wallet.

Past another phalanx of grain elevators, he found himself in front of a sign with two arrows at the lower end of a bridge that went over the train tracks. The arrow pointing left was next to the words *Business District.* The arrow pointing to the right was next to the word *Canada.*

Ry headed for the business district. It was the old downtown. About half of it was boarded up. Of the other half, what was still open at this time of day was bars. He decided to try the next block over. The movie theater was open. He could even afford it, but it might not be the smartest move. When he came out, it would be night, full on.

He soon walked into a welcoming neighborhood of tidy houses with trees and bushes and vacu-formed and extruded plastic toys in cheerful, noxious colors sprinkled across the yards. Ry felt he was walking into a club of which he was a member, and he walked down the sidewalk with some confidence that no one glimpsing him through a front window, with the distance of a front yard separating them, would take any notice of him. (He was forgetting a few aspects of his current appearance.)

It was not the kind of club where he could walk up and knock on someone's front door, though. Not like in the very olden days when travelers were taken in (and fed) by total strangers.

He had never before studied a street in terms of the places it provided for shelter. The pickings were slim. Maybe after everyone went to bed, he could sit on someone's porch. He walked up one street and down another, the streets filled with houses. The houses were filled with people who had lives and families and friends, but he had no connection to any of them.

The houses had windows that were beginning to glow, golden with lamplight or blue with TV light, as dusk sifted down. Whiffs of dinners, wafts of conversation murmured through the air—good smells, friendly sounds, but he had to keep walking as if he had somewhere to go.

How good it would feel if one of the houses would take him in. If a door opened and a familiar voice called out, "Ry! Get in here! Where have you been?"

He decided to go back to the street with the bars. At least he could get a burger or something. But he had turned a few corners and, trying to retrace his steps, he must have missed a turn. Because here was a park, with a gazebo. He was pretty sure he hadn't passed that before. Or this school. Or this church, with its yellow bricks illuminated by lights hidden in the shrubbery.

Other than the gazebo park and the school and the church, the rows of houses and trees might as well have been twenty-foot-high hedges in a maze. Ry was the rat, searching for his cheese. Burger. The tired, hungry rat.

All of the people seemed to have gone inside. For dinner, no doubt. Chicken, maybe, or spaghetti. Up ahead, though, a guy was in his driveway, doing something with a truck and a welding torch. In the fading light, it was hard to make out what he was doing, exactly, but it looked like he had chopped apart a couple of pickup trucks and was welding them together in a new way. The cab of one pickup truck now rested somehow on top of the walls of the box of another pickup. Both pickups had the rounded shape and the aura of automotive ancientness. The guy who was welding had his back toward Ry. As Ry approached in his weakened, famished state, he fell under the spell of the welding torch and he stopped, transfixed by the flame and the sparks flying into the onset of a night that had no place for him. He thought he might watch, just for a minute or two, and he sat down, almost without realizing it, on a small stack of tires that some lobe of his desperate mind had noticed.

Once he sat down, it seemed unlikely that he would be standing up anytime soon. The streetlights flickered on, and one of them lit Ry up like a lone actor on a stage. But still, he didn't move. He couldn't move.

The welder took his mask off, then. He noticed Ry, and nodded. He worked for a few minutes longer, putting his tools in order. He saw that Ry was still sitting there, and said, "How's it going?"

Ry opened his mouth for the word *okay* to come out. Instead, his lips lost their ability to form that word, or any word. A sound issued from his throat, but it left his mouth unshaped. Tears were forming and welling up in his eyes. He clenched his jaw and fixed his gaze on the odd-looking truck in an effort to stop the tears from spilling out onto his cheeks. He focused on the truck.

The two trucks. Seeing, without seeing, the door handles, the bumper, the dull red spots of primer, a sticker on a window.

"What're you doing?" he croaked finally. He was embarrassed by his voice, but relieved that he had managed to speak. He cleared his throat and said, "I mean, it looks cool, but can you actually drive it, on regular roads?"

By the end of the sentence, his voice sounded almost normal. Normal was what he was going for. Forgetting, just briefly, how not ordinary it was to materialize in a total stranger's driveway at nightfall, filthy and bruised and on the verge of tears, in a torn bloody T-shirt, wearing only one shoe.

Del had taken note of all this while Ry was gazing fixedly at the truck. He guessed at Ry's age—fourteen? Fifteen? And wondered who had roughed him up. He wondered if the boy would tell him. "How's it going?" had apparently been way too intrusive. Maybe he was hungry. Maybe the best thing would be to feed him.

"I was just about to go get a bite to eat," he said. "Have you eaten?"

"You mean, like, today?" asked Ry.

"I mean, like, recently," said Del.

"No," said Ry. "I had breakfast."

"Okay," said Del. "Wait a minute." He opened one of the truck doors, leaned inside, and emerged with a clean, folded T-shirt and a pair of flip-flops.

"Here," he said. "Put these on. We're not going anyplace fancy, but your shirt's looking a little unappetizing, and you need to have shoes on both feet. My name is Del."

"I'm Ry," said Ry.

"Do you want to go inside and wash up first?" asked Del. "The bathroom is straight ahead."

Ry had never before been so happy about soap and warm water, and then a towel. He felt like singing. But didn't. He examined his reflection in the mirror. It was true that his T-shirt was now a shredded dirty rag. Looking down, he remembered that it was bloodstained, too, from his nose. He pulled it off and put on the fresh one, which was tan and had a picture of a tree on it.

He checked himself out in the mirror again, this time admiring his blossoming black eye. His eyeball blinked back at him through a crevice in the swollen discolored hillock that was now the most striking feature of his sunburned face. Kind of cool looking except that it hurt. A dull ache with a throb.

It occurred to him that the mirror was the door of a

medicine cabinet. On the premise that medicine cabinets were like bathrooms in fast food restaurants—a shared resource for the common good—he opened the door. There was a razor and a shaving brush. Toothpaste and toothbrush. Earwax removal fluid. A jar of Vaseline. A bottle of generic aspirin that had two tablets left.

Ry hesitated. He put the bottle back on the shelf and closed the door.

The velvet black sky was crammed thick now with stars. And the air was chilly, especially on sunburned flesh. Ry shivered, and put his hands as deep in his pockets as they would go. His bare toes and heels hung over the edges of the flip-flops. They looked like girl flip-flops. Kind of skinny, and they were turquoise. Del came out of the garage, pulled the door down, and nodded toward the truck.

"Hop in," he said. "Let's see if we can drive it on a regular road."

Climbing up into the old truck was like stepping into a time machine. The worn leathery seat and the spacious darkness of the cab, with lighted dials glowing from the dashboard, lighting the rounded edges of knobs and levers, gave off an immense feeling of safety. Ry wanted to stay there forever, except that he was starving. His stomach was now making the cartoon sound effects for two space aliens having a fistfight. Or whatever kind of fight they had.

"What are you doing to this truck?" he asked again. "I mean, why are you putting the other truck on top of it?"

"Everyone wants to ride in the front seat," said Del. "Everyone wants to look out the front window."

"How will people get up there?" asked Ry.

"I haven't quite figured that out," said Del. "But I'm working on it. I have some ideas."

"Do you have a big family?" asked Ry. Because he was wondering who "everyone" was, who needed to have seats in the front.

Del considered the question before answering.

"Not strictly speaking," he said. "Do you?"

"No," said Ry. "Just my mom and dad. And our dogs. And my grandpa." Mentioning them was like looking down from the tightrope, remembering the precariousness of his situation, losing his balance. Looking up, he saw that they were pulling into a small gravel parking lot alongside a boxy gray building.

"Do they know where you are?" ventured Del as they got out of the truck. The doors ka-thunked shut, they walked the short distance to the restaurant.

"I don't even know where I am," said Ry.

The restaurant had a theme of mining. There was a framed brownish photograph of old-time guys with suspenders and brimmed hats standing at the opening to a mine, right inside the door, and a pickax and shovel hanging from the wall behind the counter. Aside from that, the theme of the place was brown. Even if your eyes were closed, the tiny molecules of gravy and meat, the golden brown molecules of the crust of rolls and of French fries, suspended in the air as thick aroma, would tell you that.

Eyes open, there was brown paneling on the wall, wood-grain Formica tabletops, an all-over brownness. With white lighting: bare fluorescent tubes over the counter and fake oil lanterns on the tables. It was nice. Not like his own home, but homey somehow.

Del asked the waitress to bring a Baggie filled with ice, and as Ry held it over his eye, he told Del how he had come to be there. Through his other eye, and through a rising tide of tiredness, Del went in and out of focus.

There was a plaid shirt, sandy wisps of hair, a face that seemed old and young at the same time. The hands lifting his fork or his coffee cup were strong, battered hands that worked hard and could do things.

The eyes that listened from beneath craggy brows

were serious or amused, but unfazed. No big deal. As if these things happened all the time. Bad luck about losing your shoe, though.

Ry told his story between bites of a roast beef sandwich with gravy on it, mashed potatoes, applesauce, buttered rolls. The warm, soft food in his mouth and stomach made up a warm, soft featherbed for his mind to crawl into. Del listened as Ry's sentences lost their endings, then their middles, then refused to start up at all. He watched as Ry's eyes tried to stay open, his head tried to stay upright on his neck, a bowling ball on a stem, but his wavering eyelids fell to, his head wilted down onto his chest with all the weight of gravity.

Del slid out from his side of the booth and guided Ry into a lying-down position so that he wouldn't fall into his food. Ry's eyes fluttered open. He said, "I have some money in my wallet."

"Don't worry about it," said Del, but Ry didn't hear him. He was already out. Del returned to his seat to finish his meal. The waitress, warming his coffee, said, "So, who's this, Del—a nephew?"

"I don't exactly know," said Del. "He showed up in my driveway. I thought he might be a runaway, but he's got some other story."

# IN THE NIGHT

He could hear a heated conversation in hushed voices. Ry couldn't make out the words, but the sound of it was vehement. And interrupted here and there by clattering mechanical cascades of . . . of what?

Straining to hear, he woke himself halfway. His eyes were still closed, but he could sense light through his eyelids. He felt the cushion his back was pressed against, his cramped position, how his bent knees cantilevered out over open air, and he thought he must be lying on a couch, and that the couch was not long enough. His shoulder was cold; pulling the something that covered him up higher, to his chin, he could tell that it was an afghan-y something, textured like that, and with places his finger poked through. It was still warm, though, even with the little holes.

The people were arguing again. They were in the

room, whatever room it was, with him. But not right next to him, maybe across the room. Ry cracked open his left eye, the uninjured one that was closer to the couch, hidden in the recesses of a pillow. A couch-y pillow.

His part of the room was in darkness, but a few yards beyond his feet was an alcove where a shaded lamp hung low over a small table. A man was sitting at the table typing on an old-fashioned typewriter. He paused in his typing and rolled the paper up in the machine to read it.

Glasses rested midway down his nose, which in profile was mildly beaklike. Wisps of hair, catching the lamplight, glowed golden. Ry knew the man from somewhere, but could not think, in his grogginess, from where. It came to him that the man's name was Del. He was making a hazy connection between the clattering sound and the old typewriter when the guy named Del erupted into a quiet but fierce argument. With . . . himself? He held his hands out, palms up, a plea for understanding. Then stubbornly folded his arms and sat back, defiant in his chair. Speaking to the air. In the tone you would use if you knew someone was sleeping nearby, but you really had to make your point. The person you were talking to would have to be right in front of you, trying to read your lips and string together the *t*'s and *p*'s and *k*'s as you told him (or her) the urgent thing that couldn't wait, that had to be said *now*. But the other person wasn't there.

Then somehow, without moving from his chair, Del was the other person, arguing back. Patiently explaining. Ry watched from the darkness of the living room. Not moving. At all. Wanting Del not to be nuts. Something else could be happening. Del could just be going over something that had happened, some conversation. Ry had done that, where you come up, hours or days later, with what you should have said, and you say it aloud. He usually said it to the bathroom mirror. In the daytime. With no one around. But everyone is different.

Or maybe what Del was typing was a play, maybe he was acting out the parts. But in the strangeness of night and the blurriness of being only half awake, Ry didn't want to think it out; he just wanted it not to be happening. He was about to pull the afghan up over his head when Del abruptly stood up, threw his hands in the air in exasperation, turned off the light, and walked out of the room. For some moments, light and muttering came from further off, then it was silent and dark and Ry would have thought about it some more, tried to figure it out, but with all the silence and darkness, it wasn't long before he slipped back into sleep.

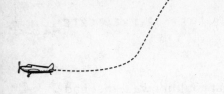

# EVERYTHING
# SEEMS MORE
# NORMAL
# IN THE MORNING

When Ry woke again, it was to the muffled sound of snoring, and the air in the room was a dim gray. He lay there as the light gathered, taking in his surroundings. The events of the day before gathered, too, in his mind. They seemed too unlikely to be true. But here he was. Which was where, exactly?

His eyes fell on an old typewriter, and it stirred something, but it was an elusive something, like a dream you can't catch before it slips away. Ry padded around the room wrapped in the afghan he had slept under. The furniture seemed old-fashioned, but not as old as really antique furniture. Not carved wood or velvety. Just mismatched and out of style, like yard sale stuff.

A pile of photographs crowded together on top of a low bookshelf, some in frames and some loose. Several were of groups of people smiling at the camera while mountains or sand dunes or glaciers or jungle-entwined Mayan ruins loomed around them. A few were of Del and other people dangling on ropes, from a tree or from a face of rugged rock into space. Ry looked at the group photos again, and found Del in each of them, at the edge or in the background, a little apart. There was one of Del sitting on a couch laughing as children crawled all over him.

A black-and-white photo of a woman, unframed and curling, sat tucked among the others. Ry picked it up and uncurled it to look at it more closely. The woman wore a costume, a Three Musketeers sort of costume, with high boots and poufy pants, poufy sleeves, and a laced vest. She must have been acting in a play; it was the kind of posed photograph with a blank background that would be in a newspaper or on a poster. In one hand she held a fencing sword. Her body was turned to the side, ready for action, but she looked over her shoulder into the camera, and her stance and her face somehow showed high drama and, at the same time, that it was all a big joke.

She was pretty. Her eyebrows had something to do with it. Her eyes almost seemed to be two different colors, but in a black-and-white photo it was hard to tell. It might have been the lighting. Ry turned the photo over. A felt-tip scrawl said, "Del—yours forever. Just kidding. No, really. Yulia."

He looked at the front again and said the name aloud, but softly, trying it out. Yulia. It was a funny name. Not funny funny, but unusual. He went to put the photo back where he had found it, but he couldn't quite remember now where that had been. He hesitated, photo in hand, trying to recall it, until he noticed a shape stenciled out of the light film of dust that lay over the shelf and everything on it. That was the spot.

Still in investigative mode, he tiptoed over to the table with the typewriter and sat in the chair. He had never used this old-timey kind. Experimentally, he touched one of the keys. You could push it down pretty far without anything actually happening, and then, suddenly, it made that metallic punching sound and the whole thing jumped slightly and Ry pulled his hand back as if he had been stung and realized with dismay that he had typed a *j* onto the paper, just below what looked like a poem. He froze, listening, but after a short pause, the snoring started up again. He noticed a small plastic bottle of correction fluid beside the typewriter. He read the directions, gave the little bottle a shake, and carefully applied a little blob of the white stuff over the *j*. It didn't dry immediately. While he waited, he looked at what was typed onto the top part of the paper.

Try as I might
I can't escape gravity.
My orbit is elliptical:
I fling myself far and think I'm free.
Who am I kidding?
Invisible forces, and visible ones,
Pull me back.
j

It looked like a poem, but it was about gravity and elliptical orbits. Okay.

Even when the Wite-Out was dry, Ry saw that it didn't match. There it was, a grayer patch over a still visible *j*. He put on another coat. He considered typing the whole thing over, but that would definitely make too much noise.

You could still see it. Oh, well. He rolled the paper back down a few notches. Maybe Del would think he did it himself, in the middle of the night. Maybe he wouldn't even notice it.

# DEL'S KITCHEN

Leaving the scene of the crime, Ry rose from the chair and went into the kitchen. Brown-and-white-checkered curtains hung neatly in front of the window over the sink, where dishes soaked in cloudy water.

The counter held a variety of condiments, empty cans, and surprisingly pretty things, like a flowered china sugar bowl and salt and pepper shakers in the shape of a little Dutch boy and girl leaning forward to kiss each other.

Ry pulled his sleeping cell phone from his pocket and woke it up. It gave forth its swirling musical greeting, friendly and reassuring. But too loud in the quiet house, like a morning person when you aren't one. His thumb immediately went for the mute button and he said, "Shhh!"

There was one bar of reception, one bar of battery. Two texts from Jake, who was still bored. One from Amanda: *Haha, how would I know?*

He called his grandfather first. Listened to the ringing, then his own recorded voice again on the voice mail. As he left his message, speaking softly, he heard his phone peeping at him, warning him that it would give up the ghost any second now. His parents' cell phone rang and rang, until the robo voice said the number was unavailable and to try again later. And the phone expired in his hand.

Ry's eyes wandered around the little room and fell on the pots and pans sitting on the stove top. Each held food remains so aged that only an archaeologist or a forensic scientist would be able to identify them. Because his mind was *a.* in a problem-solving mode, and *b.* easily distracted, he proceeded to solve the four puzzles.

The dried brown stuff looked like the dried brown stuff in the can that said "Beef Stew." The dried greenish stuff went with the stuff in the can that said "Split Pea Soup." The dried reddish-brown stuff had probably started out as spaghetti sauce. The bumps in it might have been meat and onions at some point in time. Easy.

Ry leaned over to look more closely at a skillet on one

of the back burners. Whatever was in it had been there long enough to accumulate dust. He didn't notice that the snoring had stopped. The sun flooded suddenly between the curtains, blinding him briefly so he didn't see Del materialize in the still shadowy margins of the room.

He had lifted the skillet into the shaft of sunlight and was considering giving it a sniff when Del spoke, and Ry's feet left the ground and the skillet left his hand and a gurgling noise came out of his throat. He landed before the skillet, which unfortunately flew off at an angle in the direction of Del's chest. Amazingly, Del put his hand right up and caught it, as if Ry had tossed him a softball.

What Del had said when he first spoke was, "I guess it's been a while since I did the dishes." At least that's what he started to say. He stopped midway when the skillet came flying toward him. What he said after he caught the skillet and looked into it was "Maybe we'd better just go out for breakfast."

## STRANGERS,
## RIDES,
## AND CANDY

In the light of day, the backyard had appeared. It was full of old trucks and machinery and large shapes covered by tarps. The seat in the truck was cold, but Ry was beginning to think of it as his. Sometimes, when something really out of the ordinary happens, like you get off your train and it leaves without you and you trudge for hours without food through an alien landscape, the things that happen after that can seem less strange just by comparison. Your threshold of what makes "strange" is raised way up for a while.

Del took a tin of mints from his pocket, opened it, and popped one into his mouth.

"Mint?" he asked Ry.

Ry realized he hadn't brushed his teeth for about twenty-four hours, was suddenly aware of a furriness inside his mouth. He wondered how foul his breath was.

"Thanks," he said, and took one.

"Strangers offering rides and candy" didn't occur to him. Only, I have to get a toothbrush. And toothpaste. But Del will probably let me use his toothpaste.

"Do you have a cell phone charger?" he asked Del. "My phone is completely dead."

Rides, candy, and cell phone chargers. But Del didn't have one.

"I don't have a cell phone," said Del. "But I know people who do. Or you can just use my regular phone."

"It would be long-distance," said Ry. "But I have some money. I could pay you."

"Doesn't matter," said Del. "Don't worry about it."

"You don't have a cell phone?" asked Ry. "Really?"

"I'm waiting to see if it's a fad," said Del.

## NEW PÊCHE SKILLET
## ("PESH")

The old truck grumbled into the gravel parking lot of the same gray-box restaurant they had been to the night before. Painted wooden letters Ry hadn't noticed the first time, although they were two feet high and painted fluorescent orange, identified it as the New Pêche Skillet. He thought he remembered Del telling him, before he zonked out, that New Pêche, pronounced "New Pesh," was the name of the town they were in. *Pêche* was French for "peach," but no one knew why it was called that. There weren't any peach trees here to speak of.

As their heels hit the ground, they were pleasantly assailed, ambushed, by the ambrosial aromas of breakfast seeping out of the building. Soon after sliding into a booth, they were joined by two people. One was a tall, rangy, cream-colored guy whose hair frizzed forth from his scalp and his chin in a brown cloud, vaporizing into thin air at his shoulders. The other fellow was short and round and coffee colored, with a shaved head.

The hairy one shook Ry's hand and said he was Pete. The sleeves of Pete's T-shirt had been hacked away, taking part of the body of the shirt with them. Revealing that Pete's armpits could keep up with his head and his chin, hair-wise. Also revealing that while Pete was lean, he was muscular. So muscular that Ry expected the handshake to be bone crushing and was grateful when he only had to wince slightly.

The short guy's name was Arvin. His T-shirt was immaculate. It looked as if it had been ironed, and it was tucked into crisp blue jeans that were folded up at the bottoms in tall cuffs. His glasses were small gold-rimmed circles, in front of eyes that moved independently of each other so that Ry wasn't sure which eye he should look at. Arvin's smile was kind, easy, and radiant. He acknowledged Del's introduction with a quick nod.

The tree image that was printed on both men's shirts was the same as what was on the shirt Del had given Ry to wear. He gathered from their preliminary bits of conversation that they worked for Del, and that having breakfast here was how they started out their day.

Looking at his own shirt, reading upside down, he read, THINK TWICE TREE SERVICE. Below the tree, in smaller letters, were the words *If you really feel it's necessary.*

Suddenly there was a hand in front of him, a beautiful hand that was connected to the arm of a young woman, who said, "I'm Beth. And you are?"

Something about her bespoke spacious skies, fruited plains, and amber waves of grain. Abundance and freshly baked bread, still warm. Maybe that part was the restaurant. Ry felt his own face grow warm. He shook her hand. It was soft, warm, and firm. He said, "Ry. My name's Ry."

"Hi, Ry," said Beth. Then she told Pete to move over so she could sit down. And he did. Beth was wearing a tree service shirt also.

No one asked Ry what he was doing there. And he was the only one who picked up a menu. He studied it as the heavenly breakfast smells and the noisy breakfast clatter and conversation enveloped him, knowing he had some money in his pocket but not knowing what else he would need to spend it on. He settled on oatmeal, because it was cheap and it would make him feel full. Arvin ordered oatmeal, too. Ry wondered if it was for the same reason, or if Arvin actually wanted oatmeal.

When the food arrived, Ry stirred butter and sugar and cream and a pinch of salt into his oats. Arvin stirred ketchup into his. Ry couldn't help staring, and Arvin laughed softly.

"Try it sometime," he said. "It's not that bad."

"Mmm," he said as he took a bite. "Mmm, mmm, mmm."

Across the table were steaming heaps of eggs, bacon, potatoes, sausage. In trying not to look at the food he wasn't eating, Ry found himself looking at the tattoos on Pete's arms. There were two, one per arm.

A colorful dragon was entwined like a magnificent 2-D pet around one arm. The tip of its tail pointed at Pete's shoulder. It breathed orange and yellow flames onto his wrist. On the other arm was a coiled snake and the words DON'T TREAD ON ME. Or was it—wait—there was a *t* missing. Whoever had done the tattoo had left out the second "t." It would be an easy mistake to make, you might be doing one *t* and your mind would go on to the next letter. The words on the scroll said, DON'T READ ON ME.

Ry's grandfather, Lloyd, took his first cup of coffee out onto the screened porch, sat down on a glider, and waited in the dark for the birds to start chirping. Between him and the sun, there was a thin bit of earth and a thick wall of trees, still black with night. As he sipped, the first rays of the sun found tiny gaps to poke through. Tomorrow he would pour the pot of coffee into a thermos to bring out onto the porch so he didn't have to go back inside.

He went into the kitchen and Olie, the black dog, went into his downward-dog yoga position, wagging his tail. Peg, the red one (or was it the other way around?), tap-danced into the room and then in a circle.

"Oh, yes, right," said Lloyd. "Well, let's go then. I don't know how you make it all night. I certainly couldn't."

He took the leashes from their hooks and, after some

fumbling, clipped them to the dogs' collars, and they headed out the door. The street was quiet. The air was cool but warming, the sky clear as it lightened. Lloyd realized he had forgotten the plastic poop bags and hoped the dogs would hold out until the woods at the end of the street. He was out of practice at this job. It had been a while since he had a dog himself. If this house-sitting pet-care stint worked out, though, he might get one.

The asphalt crumbled off into dirt, and he followed the dogs' bouncing butts up the path. They reminded you that it was fun to be alive. They investigated everything; they *liked* to move. And they could spend a lot of time sleeping. That would work out well for him, too.

Birds chattered in the treetops. Lloyd tried to imagine what a path looked like to a dog. The woods were so open here, they could have trotted in any direction they wanted to. He decided it had to do with smells; they were following the scent of previous walkers, human and canine.

A squishy crunch led him to find that he had exterminated a snail. He began to look more at where he was putting his feet. In this way he soon saw a lovely little toad, which he was very happy not to have stepped on. As well as the excreted or regurgitated version of a small furry animal. Who was responsible for that, he wondered. After that, he only looked down enough not to step on something. Or someone.

A pair of black squirrels raced fearlessly along the most tenuous, slender limb and leaped, one after the other, from that limb to an equally untrustworthy-looking limb on a neighboring tree. Did they ever miss? If he were a squirrel, he might just scamper along the ground and then crawl into his cozy nest. He had heard on the radio that squirrels could live to be twenty-five years old. While rats lived only to the age of three. Twenty-five years seemed like a long time to be a squirrel.

The dogs stopped in their tracks. Following their gaze, Lloyd saw that a doe, equally as still, gazed back. For a magical instant, the four creatures observed one another. Then the doe bounded off in that how-does-such-a-large-animal-move-so-fast-and-yet-so-silently-and-with-such-grace kind of way, and the dogs took after her raised white flag, slobbering panting buffoons crashing through the undergrowth. Lloyd saw it coming. He clicked down on the buttons of the retractable leashes and braced himself, but he was dragged along like a water-skier. He laughed as he tried to slow the dogs down, hopping over fallen branches and ducking under low-hanging ones, picking his feet up and putting them down more rapidly than he had done lately.

It didn't take long for the doe to outwit the dogs. She evaporated, and they sniffed the air in all directions. Then, forgetting her, they turned their noses to other fascinating scents in the nearby grasses. Lloyd was still smiling as he watched them and waited for his breathing and his heart to settle back to normal. Maybe if he got a dog, it should be an older dog. A slower dog. One with a touch of arthritis.

They had bolted into a clearing. A pile of melon-sized rocks suggested that someone had once prepared the field for planting, but now it had the air of a long-forgotten place. Lloyd remembered that he had left the coffeemaker on. He had a hankering for that second cup. He clicked his tongue to tell the dogs it was time to go. They pranced back and forth ahead of him, heading back toward the trees.

And then, without warning, the earth fell away, far away, from beneath his feet, and he plummeted after it. The earth fell eight feet down before it stopped falling, and so did Lloyd. When he stopped moving, he was lying in the bottom of a sinkhole twenty feet across. The dogs looked down at him from the rim.

Here's what had happened: The bedrock below the soil and glacial deposits he was standing on was limestone, with fissures and layers that water could seep through. As the water seeped, it dissolved more and more of the limestone until it was more air and water than solid. Eventually, i.e., at that very moment, there just wasn't enough rock to hold up the dirt anymore. So the dirt collapsed.

It was unlikely that Lloyd would happen to be standing exactly there when the dirt collapsed, but there he was. It could have been worse. It could have been a twenty-foot-deep sinkhole.

"Go get Timmy," said Lloyd to the dogs. "No, wait—I'm Timmy. Go tell June Lockhart that I've been swallowed up by the earth. She'll know what to do."

He was making a joke about a television show in the early 1960s in which a boy named Timmy was rescued every week by his collie, whose name was Lassie. The dogs didn't know about this program, and they lay down and waited. At first with their ears perked up. When they saw that Lloyd had closed his eyes, they took naps, too.

Lloyd closed his eyes because as he fell, his head had landed on a rock. The field was a pocket of glacial till, and it was about 80 percent rocks. Most of the back side of his body had also met up with rocks. But it was the meeting of a rock with his head that caused him to close his eyes. He slipped into unconsciousness, and he stayed that way for several hours. The dogs waited patiently.

# ANOTHER
# SEPARATE,
# RELATED STORY:
# SIESTA

Other than the rivulets of molten lava burping up out of occasional fissures in its crater, and the steam that rose from them, the volcano had been dormant for such a long time that tall trees grew on its steep slopes.

A few locals earned a living by leading tourists up winding paths that were almost unfindable in the undergrowth, climbing over the waist-high, even shoulder-high, banyan tree roots to the top.

When they got up there, they could look around panoramically. To the north and south, a few other tiny islands emerged from the water. To the west was the Caribbean. And to the east was the Atlantic Ocean, with nothing at all emerging from it for more than three thousand miles, only ocean until the coast of Africa, unless you were lucky enough in your swim or boat ride to hit the Cape Verde Islands, almost to Africa anyway, and here you were on this teeny-tiny island, and what if you fell off? Especially on the Atlantic Ocean side?

Then the tourists would venture into the crater and observe the glowing lava trickles and the steam, and try to remember those diagrams of volcanoes everyone had to draw in fifth grade, and wonder how dormant a volcano could be if it still had glowing lava coming out of it? Here it was, geology in real life (though geology was really *every*where; it *was* real life), and it was all pretty incredible, but it was also a relief to get back to the bottom and eat one of the sandwiches that the guide had packed, even if giant ants had found their way inside the bag and had to be brushed away.

Meanwhile, back up behind them, the thick heat of the tropical afternoon settled around the mountain. Twitters and chirps and squawks punctured the heavy stillness here and there, but it was siesta time.

The perky ringtone of a cell phone sang out into the cloud forest. No one was there to notice how the narrow rectangular window on its face lit up.

Five minutes after its Answer button went unpressed, it emitted a musical burble.

By the second burble, a small monkey with a green

cast to her fur had located the smooth silvery object. She waited for it to speak again, and it did. She touched the small bumps along the edges, and it peeped and glowed at her. And it vibrated, like a bee trapped under a leaf, tickling the palm of her hand. Foot. Whatever. She squeaked, then carried it off to show her family and friends.

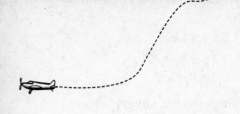

# BETTY,
# BETTY,
# BETTY

In the booth at the New Pêche Skillet, Del and Pete were having a discussion.

"I like to fly under the radar," Pete was saying.

"So, what happened to your eye?" asked Beth. She was talking to Ry.

"I just let them know where I stand," said Del. "I don't have anything to hide." He was talking to Pete.

"I walked into something," said Ry. "A big metal cable. It was in the shadow, and it was coming straight at me. I didn't see it."

"I'm not hiding anything," said Pete. "But I'm not going to broadcast it, either."

"Ow," said Beth. "You're lucky you didn't poke your eye out. Where was this cable? What were you doing?"

Bit by bit she pried it out of him. It was surreal to be

sitting in the same booth, in the same restaurant, telling the same story he had told the night before to Del. But he was awake this time. And Beth was so interested. She kept asking him questions and listening to the answers. And there were the breakfast smells and the friendly hubbub of voices and clattering dishes and clinking silverware and the sunlight pouring through the windows. . . . Ry found he was chattering away, and when he ran out of things to say, he realized that everyone in the booth was now listening to him.

"Are there any other people you could call, any other relatives?" Del asked. "Besides your grandfather?"

"Maybe a neighbor, someone who could go see if your grandfather's okay?" This was Beth.

"We just moved," said Ry. "I don't actually remember anybody's last name. There's a lady named Betty."

"Betty," said Pete. "Betty, Betty, Betty. Let's call Betty."

"I don't know her last name."

"I know, I was just—tell me again, what is the deal with your parents?"

"They're sailing around the Caribbean. I think they're revitalizing their marriage or something."

"That sounds nice," said Beth. "I'd like to do that. How long do they think it will take?"

"Take?" asked Ry.

"Do they have an itinerary?" asked Arvin. "Or are they just blowing in the wind, wherever love takes them, skipping over the ocean like a stone?"

"Arvin's kind of a mystic," explained Beth.

"Almost a monk, really," said Pete. "He's a Buddhist."

"It's words to songs," said Arvin. "The stuff they play on that radio station you people listen to."

"Oh, sorry," said Beth. "I thought you were being poetic."

"Not me," said Arvin. "Delwyn's the poet."

Ry didn't want to picture his parents letting love take them where it would. He wanted to picture them answering their phone and telling him what he should do.

"I think they have reservations at some of the places they want to stay," he said. "My grandpa has the list. But I think some of the time they're just going to sail around wherever. I feel like I should just go home. But it's kind of impossible. I only have, like, eighty-five dollars, and my return ticket is in my backpack, which is who knows where."

"Maybe he could work with us for a couple of days, Del," said Beth, "and earn his train fare. He looks like a strapping lad. And in the meantime," she said, turning back to Ry, "your grandpa will remember to check the answering machine, or he'll be there when you call. I bet he's next door, blabbing with Betty."

It was the sort of thing you say to make a person feel like he's doing something when all there is to do is wait. No one, except maybe Ry, who didn't know what would happen next, really expected him to work long enough to earn three hundred dollars, or whatever it would cost for a ticket. It was a distraction. But everyone went with it, waiting for the better idea to come along.

"We need to find him some shoes then," said Del. "He can't work in flip-flops."

"What size are you?" asked Pete.

"Ten," said Ry.

"Same as me," said Arvin. "Almost. I'm ten and a half."

"Do you have any extra shoes?" asked Pete.

"No," said Arvin. "Not work shoes."

"He needs shoes he can keep," said Beth, "to wear back on the train. We can make a quick trip to the Sally."

# (SHOES)
# (LOST AND FOUND)
# (CINDERELLA)

"The Sally" was the Salvation Army Thrift Shop. Once inside, Ry's new companions strayed like cats, every one to his own way. He stood just inside the door, bereft. Without his team buoying him along, he was less certain that what he was doing made any sense. He moved toward a set of shelves that held plates, bowls, and glasses. Kitchen things. The shelf at eye level was filled with mugs imprinted with photographs of children, grandchildren, best friends, boyfriends, and girlfriends. There were inscriptions like "World's Best (fill in the blank)", "I ♥ (whoever)", "BFF."

Abandoned now like puppies at the pound, they huddled together on the cold metal shelf. It was kind of depressing. Who was going to buy a mug with a picture of a total stranger? They were doomed. Their ranks would only grow. It would be kind of funny, though, if you had a restaurant, to use only this kind of cup. He was momentarily glad to be far from home; if he saw someone he knew on a cup, he would have to rescue it. Them.

"Ohmigod," said Beth, suddenly beside him. "Look what I found. Wait. We have to go to an outlet." She took Ry by the elbow. As she led him along, he saw that in her other hand she carried a plastic cactus in a plastic pot, with a cord attached. When they reached the wall, she plugged it in. Many of the plastic cactus bristles were optic fibers, and pinpricks of light shone from their tips in an ever-changing array of color.

"I can't believe someone would get rid of this," said Beth. "Can you?" When Ry didn't immediately respond, she said, "Picture it in the dark."

"Cool," said Ry. It would be better in the dark, he guessed, when you couldn't see the cheesy plasticness of it, just the shimmering lights.

"Okay," said Beth. "Never mind. Let's go find you some shoes."

On the way she grabbed a package of socks from a spinning rack.

Del was already in the shoe area. He was methodically checking each pair in the unmethodical aroma-of-feet jumble for size. He glanced up as they approached.

"It's not the greatest selection," he said. "But I found a few." He nodded toward three pairs he had set aside.

Ry had imagined something like the work boots Del and his crew all wore, maybe a more beat-up version of his own hiking boots. A pair of tennis shoes would have been okay. So far, his choice was between an old man's dress shoes, reddish brown; crinkly white business-lizard loafers with a gold chain on one but missing from the other, and pull-on ankle-high boots of scuffed black suede with triangular elastic inserts on the sides.

"Give those a try," said Del. "I guess you need socks, too."

"I've got some right here," said Beth, ripping open a plastic pouch. Ry pulled on the white cotton tube socks. Blue stripes went around the tops.

The ankle boots were the only pair that looked like they had been worn by a person under sixty years old, so he tried them first. He could barely get his foot inside.

Next he tried the dress shoes. They were huge. He would have been relieved about this except that it left him with the most horrible shoes, the shoes of last resort: the shiny white loafers.

Reluctantly, he slipped them on. He hated to admit it,

but this pair felt the best. They were all cushiony.

"Wow," said Beth. "You would need a lot of self-esteem to walk around in those all day."

Ry looked at his feet and legs in one of those little shoe mirrors that sat on the floor. The shoes were a metaphor for the decline of western civilization: crappy and glitzy and barely useful, but pretty comfortable. This is the narrator's opinion. Ry didn't think that thought specifically, but he felt as dispirited as if he had.

The contrast between the shoes and the striped tube socks was interesting. Probably a metaphor for something depressing, too. It looked as if a lawn mower–riding failed gambler in shorts with a potbelly should be attached to his legs. But shoes were just something to put on your feet, right? It wasn't like he had to wear these the rest of his life.

Beth, meanwhile, said, "Men don't know how to shop." She went over to see what Del had missed. When she came back, she had a pair of blue-and-yellow Pumas. They were soiled and worn, but intact.

They fit like gloves. Whatever that means when you're talking about shoes. They fit like magic slippers, in a fairy tale.

"You don't have to pull the socks all the way up like

**71**

that," said Beth. She folded the tops over and smooshed them down. "There," she said.

Ry felt almost normal. He looked at Beth with gratitude. She was pleased, too.

"I know," she said. "I'm amazing."

Pete and Arvin had materialized. Pete held a cookie jar shaped like a parrot. Arvin carried a teakettle.

"Thoreau said to beware of enterprises that require new clothes," said Pete.

"But did he say you have to go barefoot?" asked Beth. "I don't think so."

"I don't think those shoes count as new," said Arvin.

"Did Thoreau say anything about ceramic parrots?" asked Del.

"It's for my mother," said Pete. "She loves this crap. You should see her house—it's full of it."

Ry tried to picture Pete in a house full of cookie jars. He tried to picture Pete with a mother. It wasn't what you thought of when you first looked at him. That would be more like, I hope he doesn't hurt me. Okay, not really— that was an exaggeration.

He tried, in his mind's eye, to morph Pete into Pete's mother. He made him smaller, rounder, and softer, and eliminated the facial hair. He pulled the rest of the hair into a ponytail and gave her sleeves. She only came up to Pete's shoulder.

"Oh my God, Pete," she said. "That is too cute. I love it!" Her voice was gravelly, like Pete's. He gave her his own mother's voice instead. It didn't quite fit, but it made her seem very motherly.

Thinking of his mother's voice made him think of his mother. He thought of how she looked when he said something she thought was funny. At first her face stayed the same, except for her eyes. They would twinkle. Then the shape of her mouth and cheeks would shift almost imperceptibly into her secretly amused expression. It was weird not to know where she was. She didn't know where he was, either. Both of them sort of thought they did, but in a useless, nonspecific way. Like, oh, yeah, my needle is right over there. In that haystack.

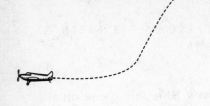

## AT
## THE
## TRAIN
## STATION

The ticket agent listened to Ry's story.

"Wow," he said. "That's a good one. Creative. But with a lot of realistic details."

"I didn't make it up," said Ry. "It's what happened."

The agent looked at Beth. With interest.

"Who are you?" he asked.

"A friend," she said. "Actually, we just met this morning. But we're already good friends. He's telling the truth. Can't you just, like, switch his ticket on your computer from August whenever to sometime this week?"

Beth was a warm and vibrant and infectious person, though *infectious* is a weird word when you think about it. Ry could tell the agent liked her, too. This made him hopeful.

The agent smiled. But it was not the smile of yes, all right, okay. It was the smile that went along with, "I'd like to help you. I really would. But I can only give him a ticket if you're such good friends that you want to pay for it."

"He already paid for a ticket," persisted Beth. "He just wants to switch it."

"He has no ID," said the agent. "What happens when someone named Ry—what is it? Wilco? Whitcomb? Wooster?—shows up in August and his ticket has been canceled?

"I'm sorry," he said. "I really am."

The only thing he was sorry about, Ry could tell, was disappointing Beth.

"Okay," said Beth, sweetly crestfallen. "Well . . . we might be back later."

"I hope so," said the agent.

"Prick," muttered Beth as they walked out the door of the station.

"There really wasn't anything he could do," said Ry.

"I like you, Ry," said Beth. "You're a good egg."

"Thanks," said Ry. He wanted to say something nice back, but he couldn't decide what.

Leaving Amtrakland, they passed a fountain, splashing the granite pant legs of the statue of some historic guy. It looked like he had gone wading.

# OOPS

$R_Y$ shinnied his way out along the limb to the place where he would tie the rope. It was the only limb that remained on this side of the tree. One by one, section by section, they had brought down the limbs below this one. First they harnessed them with ropes, then they chopped them, then the chunks fell, more or less, right where Del wanted them to fall. Arvin chopped them into smaller chunks, and Ry and Beth carried them to the back of Pete's pickup.

They were taking the tree down because it was dying, and big heavy parts of it were hanging over two houses and a garage. The idea was to get it down before those parts fell off and knocked holes through someone's roof. And to not drop parts of it on someone's roof while they were getting it down. So far, so good. It was work, but it was also a game. A large game. Del was the only one who completely understood the rules. The others sort of understood. Ry got that there were rules, and he saw that there was a logic to them, but he could see that it would take a while to really get the hang of it. Still, after watching Pete crawl out on a few limbs, he thought he'd like to try. So Del hooked him up and explained what he was supposed to do. Which was to creep out onto this limb with a coil of rope hooked to his waist.

He couldn't help noticing how high up in the air he was. Higher than the roofs of any nearby houses. His knees were bent and his feet were hooked onto the limb behind him, his thighs clamped in a vise-grip around it. Like a witch riding a broomstick. Except not moving forward as fast. Like a cross between a witch and a caterpillar. He looked into the eyes of a hawk as it soared past. His coworkers moved around like ants, far below. Okay, not ants. But chipmunks. It was pretty far down.

He focused again on the limb ahead of him. The texture of the bark. Inching forward, he reached his spot. Now he was supposed to tie the knot. Except that to tie the knot, he would have to let go of the limb with his hands, and he found himself suddenly unable to do that.

It was the height. If he were only a few feet off the

ground, in this exact same position, he wouldn't even think about falling. He hadn't thought about it out on the other limbs. But I'm not only a few feet off the ground, he thought. It seemed certain that the instant he let go, he would topple over and go into free fall, meeting the ground with a breath-robbing, crunchy-gooey, heavy thud. He could imagine the thud. In reality, he probably wouldn't hear the thud. He would be unconscious. If he was lucky.

He decided to do as much of the operation as he could one-handed, so he could hold on with the other hand. Holding on with his left, he took the coil of rope with his right. He found the end of it and let the middle fall. Don't think about it. Think about the knot.

Ry managed most of the knot with the heels of his hands resting on the limb. When he had to lift a hand away, he made sure the other hand was holding on. He was giving the knot one last quick tug when a loud crack split the air. It was a semi-distant crack; he didn't think it had anything to do with him, though it startled him and he was already wobbly. He had both hands on the limb again, a safer feeling.

But then the limb shuddered and gave way beneath him.

Ry fell with the limb, clutching it as if it could save him. Together they fell, fell, fell. Passing before life's

eyes, because life was standing as still as a statue; it was Ry that was moving. Moving too fast. Moving down. Picking up speed.

And then he stopped.

With a jolt and a rebound, he was suddenly suspended in midair by the harness Del had made him wear. Oh, yeah! he thought. The harness! He dangled twenty feet or so above the ground. This was an estimate, based on how, as Pete and Arvin trotted over, they looked. Bigger than ants or chipmunks, but not as big as he wanted them to look, which would be actual size. Was it panic he saw on their upturned faces, or just interest? It was hard to tell from here. Through the jumble of blood crashing in his ears and his heart thumping, he heard Del's unflustered voice, off to the left somewhere, say "Oops."

Looking over, Ry saw him scamper across a roof.

"Hang on," Del called out. Ry hung on.

But now that it was detached from its tree, the tree limb was heavy, and its dead weight wanted only to crash down onto the ground. He could feel the death-grip of his knees and thighs loosening. He was going to drop it. And Pete and Arvin were directly below him, as if they meant to catch him. They were in the perfect position to be wiped out by the falling limb.

"Watch out!" Ry bellowed. "I have to let go. It's going to fall. MOVE!"

Pete and Arvin grasped the imminent threat and scattered.

Ry let go. The limb fell the rest of the way. It bounced once or twice, then lay still. Hanging in space, Ry looked down at it. Then around him, at the empty air. Farther off, he saw the gutter running along the roof edge of a two-story house, at eye level.

He hung there diagonally, balancing himself by holding fast to the ropes he was suspended by. One was tied to another tree. The other went to the remaining limb of the tree they were removing. He hoped that whatever had happened to his limb wouldn't happen to that one, too.

In an unwelcome surprise development, Ry was suddenly aware that he needed to pee. He would have to block it out. Mind over matter. Easier said than done.

Del had reached the roof edge closest to where the other rope was tied. He paused for a bare microsecond to lay out his path, his plan. Then, in one fluid movement, he lowered himself to a porch railing, reached out for a limb, hoisted himself onto another limb, took a couple of quick steps, and dropped nimbly into position within the

V of the bifurcating trunk, where he began to work the rope he had tied there.

As if he did this every day.

Maybe he did.

Ry watched in admiration. How did he do that? He felt again the extremity of his situation and murmured, "Hurry, Del." And, "Hurry faster." Glancing back down into the yard and its surroundings, he scouted for a place to go, once he landed.

He felt a movement, felt himself drop a half foot, felt his self-control struggle to recover. Del had dismantled the knot. The rope was wrapped twice around the tree, which Del was using as a pulley. His muscles and tendons bulged as he released the rope, hand over hand, a little bit at a time. He must be strong, Ry thought. I couldn't do that. But he thought he would like to be able to.

Each release of rope brought Ry that much closer to earth. Each downward jolt brought his bladder that much closer to eruption. He was almost down. His toes touched the ground. And his heels. He readied himself to dash to the spot he had chosen, a nook nestled between a fence, a bush, a storage hut, and a garbage container. He unclipped the harness, and it fell to his ankles. Beth rushed over in concern.

"Are you all right?" she asked. She put her arm around Ry's back and with her other hand clasped the arm closest to her, in the way a big sister or a mother or an aunt would. Still, Ry felt his face grow warm.

"I'm okay," he said.

Arvin and Pete had rushed over, too.

"Excuse me," Ry said. "I'll be right back." It was amazing how your brain could fill up so full of what was happening right now that it could forget all about what had happened thirty seconds ago.

## A FARAWAY BUT RELATED STORY: WISCONSIN

When Lloyd opened his eyes again, Peg licked his face. She had crawled down into the hole with him and lay close against his side, waiting for him to awaken. Olie, up on the rim, was watching something with great interest, his ears at full attention, his head shifting abruptly from side to side.

It took a few minutes for Lloyd to recollect what had happened and where he was, and another few minutes for him to decide that he'd better try to sit up. Crawling up out of the hole was not impossible, but it was awkward and tricky. There was nothing solid to grab onto, and with every other step the ground seemed to collapse into hidden, bottomless pockets.

Once he made it onto solid ground, he wanted to get clear of the treacherous field. But looking around, he saw an unbroken perimeter of maple and aspen saplings growing in tall thickets. He could not tell where they had entered. The angle of the sun told him only that time had passed. Which way was which? Then his eyes fell again on the pile of rocks and the partial foundation. He tried to recall where he was standing when he first saw them, and he went and stood in that position, not trusting the ground to stay where it was when he stepped on it. His head throbbed when he moved. The bump on the back of it was tender to the touch. Making an about-face, he tentatively headed into the trees.

Olie and Peg differed on where to go next. They wandered in opposite directions to the ends of their leashes and looked back at him. This way. No, this way. Lloyd knew the path could not be far off. He just couldn't see it. He racked his brain for some landmark he might have noticed that morning. All he came up with was twittering birds and squirrels. And then he saw what seemed to him a small miracle. A human head was bobbing along. He shouted.

# A FARAWAY BUT RELATED STORY: DOG VERSION

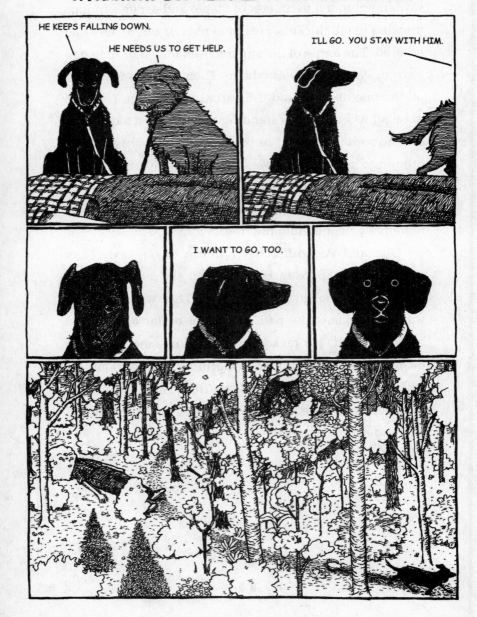

# ANOTHER FARAWAY
# BUT RELATED STORY,
# THIS ONE
# WITH A BEAUTIFUL
# SUNSET

Roughly thirty-four hundred miles to the southeast of New Pêche, the sun was setting. Ry's mother and father dangled their feet from a dock attached to an island and watched it. Once it got close to the horizon, it fell so quickly. The sky was deep blue, lavender, peach, yellow, tangerine. Just ahead of them, the shore curved around and offered up picturesque palm trees in silhouette. Gray violet cloud wisps drifted along in the distance.

"What an absolutely beautiful sunset," said Wanda.

"We should have done this years ago," said Skip.

"You're right," she said. "I just always worry—"

"You don't need to worry," he said. "Everything will be fine."

"I liked his old camp where they made them write postcards home before they could eat dinner," she said.

"Where would he send them?" asked Skip.

"I don't know," she said.

"Don't worry," he said. "Everything is fine. Nothing's going to happen."

# DOGS

# AT
# THE END
# OF THE DAY

The crew caravanned to Del's house to unload the hunks of chopped-up tree into stacks in his backyard. Ry fully intended to help out with all that, but he slipped into the house, for only one minute, to plug in his phone. In the kitchen he busted open the packaging of his new charger and scanned for an outlet. The voices of the others shuttled past the open window. Weren't there any outlets in this house? Was Del waiting to see if electricity was a fad, too?

Aha! He found one. The phone lit up. He turned to go back outside, but the phone called him back. It said there were messages. He would just check.

From Nina: *You're in Montana. Right?*

From Connor: *I don't know. So, you wanna play b-ball? Oh, wait—you moved. Duh.*

Ry gave his phone raspberries. He didn't text back. And when no one answered—grandpa, mother, father— he didn't leave a message. He stood in the dim kitchen, thinking. He had relatives, aunts and uncles. They were far away, and he didn't have their numbers with him, but they existed. He guessed that was the next thing he should do. He was starting to work it out when he heard Del's voice outside the window.

"I've been thinking about it," Del said. "I think I should just give him a ride home."

"What?" said Beth.

Ry drew closer. Beth was tossing Del chunks of wood from the bed of Pete's pickup. Del was stacking them next to the house. Their conversation was punctuated by wood falling on wood.

"I could loan him the money for a train ticket," said Del. "But it just doesn't feel right to put him on a train when we don't know for sure that someone's going to be there at the other end. I would feel responsible if something happened."

"That must be why you had him shinny out on a dead tree limb," said Beth.

"He was wearing a harness," said Del. "It was completely safe." *Ka-thunk.*

"I guess," said Beth.

"And besides, it's fun," said Del.

"Uh-huh," said Beth. "He looked like he was having a great time.

"Doesn't he live, like, a thousand miles from here?" she asked. "That's a bit of a hike."

"I was thinking of heading in that direction anyhow," said Del. "I have some errands to run out there." *Thunk.*

"Right," said Beth. "Errands. In Wisconsin." *Clunk. Chunk.*

"On the way there," said Del. "More likely on the way back. People I haven't seen for a while. It'll only take a couple of days. Three or four, round trip."

Ry stepped quietly backward into the shadowy house. He went out the backdoor, to where Pete and Arvin were ka-thunking their own pile of wood alongside the garage. He helped them stack, but his thoughts blurred out their conversation. They spoke to him a few times, and laughed when he didn't answer.

"He's somewhere else right now," said Arvin. Pete moved his hand in front of Ry's face. "Come back," he said. "Anybody there?"

Ry came back into focus. "Oh," he said. "Sorry. I was thinking about something."

"What's on your mind?" asked Arvin. "Hey . . . you all right?"

Ry needed to talk it around. So he told them about the conversation he overheard between Del and Beth.

"In a way," he said, "It would be easier for me than anything else. Otherwise, it's finding my relatives and them buying me plane tickets and flying me wherever when probably my grandpa just isn't answering the phone. I hope. But what kind of person does that? Isn't it kind of . . . extreme?"

Arvin answered first. "Only compared to most people," he said. "But that's not saying much. Delwyn is a man who likes to—how should I say it—he likes to rise to the occasion.

"Like driving you home all the way to Wisconsin. Nothing could make him happier. Unless maybe it's picking up three hitchhikers, getting a cat down out of a burning building, and rebuilding someone's transmission with nothing but a fingernail clipper along the way. Mainly I think he just wants to make sure everything's okay."

Del called to Arvin to give him a hand, and Arvin started to head over. Then, turning and smiling his big smile, he said, "Oh, yeah. Watch out for damsels in distress, or you might never get home."

Pete had something he wanted to say, too.

"It's true that Del is an unusual person," he said. "He has his own rules. You know how Thoreau talks about the guy who marches to the beat of a different drum? Well, Del marches to the beat of, like, I don't know, a harmonica or something.

"What I'm saying is, sometimes it might seem like he's out of his mind. Maybe he is, in a way. I mean, who isn't, right? But don't worry. You'll be okay."

Then he said, "Hey, I better go help those guys." And off he went.

But Beth materialized beside Ry like the third visitation, the Ghost of Christmas Future.

"Do you think Del is nuts?" Ry asked her.

"Who said that?" asked Beth.

"Pete," said Ry.

Beth snorted. "I guess he should know, right?"

"Not exactly," said Ry. "He said that Del marches to the beat of a harmonica."

Beth tilted her head back and let out a "Ha!"

"Okay," she said. "That I'll buy. That's actually pretty good."

Ry told her how he had heard Del's idea through the kitchen window. And how he didn't know what to think about it.

"Are you worried?" she asked. "Because you don't need to be." She seemed about to go on, to say something more, when Del approached and said, "Worried? What are you worried about?"

Flustered, Ry said, "I'm worried about my grandpa. How he's not answering the phone."

"Let's go find out what's going on," said Del.

"I already told him about your idea," said Beth. Just to keep things simple.

"What if something happened to him?" said Ry. "What if—?"

"Then we would have to go find your parents," said Del.

Ry looked at him. Trying to tell if Del was serious. He couldn't tell.

"I don't even know exactly where they are," he said. "There are, like, a thousand islands down there. And I don't have any money. It would be impossible."

"Uh-oh," said Beth. "Those are magic words to Del. But I don't think even you can drive to a Caribbean island, Del."

"We'd have to get to San Juan," said Del. "Then we'd have to borrow a boat."

"San Juan," said Beth. "Hmm . . . isn't that where Yulia lives?"

"It's just a hypothetical situation," said Del. "It's pretty unlikely that it would ever actually come up."

Maybe that piece of the conversation made driving to Wisconsin seem completely reasonable. Because then the talk went from whether they should go, to which vehicle they should take. Not the double-decker; there were only two of them. Del decided on a Willys. He had two. They were really old Jeep station wagons. He had modified them in a number of ways, one being that he made them longer in the back, so that two sleeping bags could fit there, stretched out full length. And he decided that, if they were going, they might as well get started. Before Ry knew it, Del had thrown the sleeping bags in and they were saying good-bye.

Beth took Ry's head between her hands and kissed him on each cheek. She was that kind of person. She also gave him a little peck on his bruised eyebrow.

"Makes you look like a tough customer," she said. Then she took his right hand in both of hers and shook it.

"Don't worry," she said, still holding on. "I'm betting everyone is fine. I bet it's just a bunch of mix-ups."

"Watch out for those damsels," said Arvin. "If you see one, make sure Del is looking the other way."

"What damsels?" asked Del.

"Just joking," said Arvin. He winked at Ry.

"Well, I guess we better go then," said Del.

And then they were going, backing out of the driveway, waving good-bye, rolling down the street. Houses, streets, minutes, and miles came and went, all ordinary enough. Ry could not identify the odd sensation he had as they rolled along. Maybe it was what a lobster feels when it finds itself in a pot of water that started out cold enough but seems to be starting to boil. Or what a snake feels as it warms on a rock, having shed the skin it has outgrown. Or maybe it was just the truck's heater in the cool of the evening. But it seemed to signal the beginning of something, a change. A sea change. Or, in this landlocked place, a shifting of the ground beneath.

Lights were appearing: headlights, dashboard lights, lights in houses. It was the hour when lights start to matter. They were exiting New Pêche almost exactly twenty-four hours after Ry had entered it. One day.

Back out into the uninhabited veldt they went. From the inside of the Willys, though, with a half-eaten Skilletburger wrapped in paper in one hand and the other half working its charms within him, the friendly thrum of the engine, another human being nearby, even scratchy music fighting its way through the airwaves and out of the old radio, the darkling world outside them seemed large and lonely in a more homey, though still mysterious way. The oncoming night blurred and swallowed up most of the vastness, leaving Ry and Del a more manageable, headlight-sized portion to deal with. Two lit cones merging into one, gray road, white and yellow traces of paint, the shoulder of gravel, dirt, and weeds. Occasionally the headlights of an oncoming car or truck appeared in the distance, grew closer, then swept by with a Doppler-ating groan.

When the burger and the cola were long gone, the darkness around the headlights was all enveloping, and focusing on the lit patch of asphalt always moving under them was like watching a scene in a movie where nothing happens, where nothing ever will happen. As if the camera was left on accidentally, pointed at nothing, and you wait for the scene to change. It was then that a picture formed itself in Ry's mind. The clutter on Del's countertop. Including his phone, plugged into the kitchen wall. Four hours behind them. He reached into his pocket.

Crap.

Is it any different to have a phone when no one you call answers, than not to have a phone at all? It did seem different. If you had the phone, there was the possibility that someone would answer, eventually. The night outside seemed blacker without it. Bleaker.

But at least they were on their way to his house.

The engine balked and stuttered, then stopped. They rolled for a short distance in silence before Del guided the truck off the road, where it came to a standstill, in the middle of the night, in the middle of nowhere.

"Damn," he said.

But he sounded happy.

# PART TWO

## IN WHICH OUR HEROES WALK DOWN THE LONELY HIGHWAY, AT LEAST ONE OF THEM HOPING FOR A RIDE

Ry opened his eyes. He pulled the warm cocoon of his sleeping bag up to his chin. The other sleeping bag was rolled up. A dream had evaporated, but not before leaving stray scraps of unease in odd places in his brain. His gaze fell, unseeing, on the faded red-and-blue flowery curtains ruched across the windows. Faint reddish light through the curtains illuminated his private capsule to the dimness of a cave or the inside of a tavern. Footfalls crunched purposefully outside, then a sound that must have been the hood of the truck being raised on unwilling hinges. Tinkering sounds—tapping, frictional, scraping, loosening, and tightening sounds.

Ry sat up, pushed open a crack between the two sides of the curtain, and peeked out. Maybe the morning light would reveal that the truck had died not far from a farmhouse or a gas station or a Burger King. But, no. He checked in three directions, the front being obscured by the raised hood. On the bright side, it looked like they were parked in a very low-crime zone. And it looked like another sunny day.

He tried to recall how they had gotten inside so he could get back out. Oh, yeah, he had to crawl up to the front seat. And there were his new old shoes. He rolled up his bag, put on the shoes and his sweatshirt, crawled over, and let himself out into the cool morning air. His own footfalls crunched purposefully away toward a stand of brush, in case a car went by, he supposed, then back to where Del stood looking at something he held in his hand.

Del reached up and pulled the hood down with a heavy thunk.

"I guess we better start walking," he said. "I think we're closer to something ahead than back. Maybe we'll pick up a ride."

Ry looked up and down the empty highway.

"It is a highway," Del said. "People do drive on it."

"Anyway," he said, a minute or two later, "I don't think we're too far from the next little town. I don't think it can be more than five miles or so."

"Five miles?" said Ry.

"That's only a couple hours' walk," said Del. "I doubt it's even that far."

Ry glanced back at the truck as they headed down the shoulder of the road. It seemed at home there in the timeless earthy expanse. It blended right in. It looked like it was planning to stay. Marry a local rock and put down roots. By the time they got back, there would probably be young tumbleweeds nesting and mating in the cab.

Del showed him the automotive object he was carrying. He had extricated it from under the hood and taken it apart. It was a generator. He explained what it did and showed Ry where the wire that wrapped around it had broken. It would have to be soldered back together. It would just wrap around one less time.

"Couldn't we sort of twist it together, like a twisty thing on a bread bag?" asked Ry.

"No," said Del, "it wouldn't be a good-enough contact. And it would be lumpy. And besides that, it would be shoddy."

He said the word "shoddy" as if it tasted bad to have it in his mouth. As if Ry had suggested taking food meant for a hungry child.

"Sorr-ree," said Ry wryly. "It was just an idea."

Del's eyes were hidden by the shadow of his sunglasses and his cap from the morning brightness that doused them from the east, but his cheeks and what Ry could see of his mouth seemed to be in the shape of being amused.

Ry didn't have sunglasses or a cap to shade his eyes, so he looked down or off to the side a lot, to avoid the glare. To the left, the north, he saw the strand of trees that meant water, a stream or a river. He thought of his lost boot. What if it was floating along right beside them? That would be kind of ironic. Maybe they should go look. Although now he didn't have the other one. He had chucked it into a trash can outside the thrift shop.

Another river thought popped into his mind, and he reached down into the corner of the cargo pocket on his shorts and fished out the little skull. He had forgotten about it. It weighed almost nothing. It was kind of amazing that he had slept in his shorts for two nights without crushing it, or feeling it.

"What kind of animal do you think this was?" he asked, handing it to Del. Del took it and looked it over with interest, but without breaking his stride.

"Where did you find it?" he asked.

Ry told him, and said, "First I wondered what

happened to him, then I wondered, why aren't there little skulls all over; why is this the only one?"

"I think nature is more efficient than we are at garbage disposal," said Del. "But it does seem like there would be more of them, like they would take a while to go away, when you think of the really old ones that they find."

Handing it back to Ry, he said, "It's not my area of expertise, but it must have been some kind of a rodent. I couldn't say what kind."

"Probably the predators chomp them right up, even their skulls," said Ry. "Probably fifty percent of what we're walking around on is undigested skull bits."

Del grinned. "You might be right about that," he said. "Though I'd prefer to think about it a little less graphically."

A spattering of cars and trucks had zipped past in one direction or the other as they walked down the road, but no one had stopped. Finally the rasp of a dragging muffler approached from behind and slowed to keep pace alongside them. The muffler trailed from the underside of a road boat, a slab on wheels, an Oldsmobile. The car rolled to a stop. It was white, with a spray of rust speckled thick across the hood where blowing sand had blasted away the paint. The window lowered and the driver leaned over and said, "You fellas need a lift?"

Del stepped up, rested his hands on top of the door, and peered in.

"Just to the next town, if you're going that far," he said. "We're having a little car trouble."

"Hop in," said the man. "You'll both have to ride up front; the backseat seems to be full."

They could see that was true; the back was piled high with cardboard cartons.

Ry slid to the middle and Del sat down beside him and pulled the door slab shut. Ry fished surreptitiously behind himself, searching for a seat belt in the crevice, but with no luck. The driver wore no seat belt and Del didn't seem to have found one either, and Ry guessed that no seat belts had been worn in this car for a long, long time.

They lurched forward and slammed to a halt to let another car fly by, then peeled out onto the highway. In no time they reached their cruising speed of Mach one. Ry was just guessing at this; the speedometer needle lay lifeless at zero. The landscape rattled by. The air-freshening cardboard pine tree jiggled a few inches in front of his nose, intertwined with a Saint Christopher's medal.

Ry slipped his hands between his knees to take up less space and to conceal his crossed fingers.

# RIDING
# WITH
# CARL

Their host was Carl. Wooly coils of silvery-white hair forested the back and sides of his head, thinning to a zone of barren scrub at the tree line of the shiny dome of his head. His mustache was waxed into handlebars. He was comfortably rounded, like a small planet, with an atmosphere made up of warmth and good humor and aftershave.

"So," he asked, "are you from around here, or just passing through?"

He wanted to hear all about their car trouble and where they were headed and where they were from. When they told him, he said, "Is that right." Or, "Isn't that something." As if it was the most interesting thing he had come across yet.

The sediment of dirt deposited evenly across the

windshield, punctuated by the dried fluids of unfortunate insects, glowed incandescent in the sunlight. It was like trying to see through dandelion fluff.

Carl fiddled with the wiper wand until a spit's worth of fluid came out and the wiper blades did their best to spread it around. This smeared the dirt into a translucent blindfold. Although it did clear off a few small areas to almost-transparency. Ry hoped Carl could see through them.

"It's all right," said Carl calmly. "I can look out the sides. We're okay so long as we stay between the ditches."

He leaned out the window.

"I can't see much anyway," he said, just as cheery. "Cataracts."

Ry noticed that though they were staying between the ditches, they were drifting from side to side, all the way across the road. He couldn't see out the front, but he could see that sometimes there was a lane to their left, sometimes to the right. And he felt the physical sensation of veering one way and then the other. There wasn't a whole lot of oncoming traffic, but still. It made him nervous. He glanced at Del, but Del was leaning out of his window, looking into the distance. Ry wondered how Carl had seen the two of them in the first place. He had to be able to see pretty decently for that, right?

Carl leaned out his window, too, squinting into the brightness. The moving air lifted clumps of his hair so that he resembled an elderly sheep, face into the wind. Drawing his head back inside, he asked Ry again where they were from, and where they were going. When Ry mentioned the car trouble, his kindly features were gently shaded with concern.

"Is that right," he said. "Isn't that something."

"You're all clear to get back in the right-hand lane now," said Del.

They meandered into their own lane in time to dodge an oncoming tractor trailer. The driver blasted his horn as he brushed past.

"That was a little close," said Del.

"I've had a lot of close calls." Carl smiled. He seemed to be untroubled by their brush with disaster.

"When you're in the service, you never know what's going to happen next," he said. "You get used to it."

"What branch?" asked Del.

"Marines," said Carl. "Korea. The infamous winter of 1950. Below-zero temperatures for weeks, in leather shoes. We were on the front lines, so we couldn't even have fires. To this day, I have no feeling from the knees down."

He looked at them, and Ry could tell Carl had just let them in on what had been an unimaginably grueling part of his life: a cold, cold fire that he had passed through, a crucible that had formed him. You had to respect that. At the same time, Ry wished mightily that he were not captive, maybe soon to be a casualty, in a car being hurled headlong down the road by a guy who couldn't see much, who couldn't remember what you said two minutes ago, and who had just told you that he had no feeling in the part of his body he was driving the car with.

Ry's mouth opened and he said, "Huh."

Carl had to be fibbing, or at least exaggerating. He had to have some feeling in his foot to keep it pressed down on the gas pedal. Especially at the speed they were going. Though maybe a lead foot and a dead-weight foot were about the same. He glanced down at Carl's senseless foot. It was wearing a bedroom slipper. One of those corduroy ones designed to look like a loafer. Pajama pants peeked out from under his trouser legs.

"So," said Carl brightly, "are you from around here, or just passing through?"

The car drifted into the westbound lane and continued

there. Maybe it was easier for Carl to go straight if he could see the edge of the road. Up close.

Del was still hanging out the window, peering down the road. Ry guessed that his plan was to be Carl's eyes and nudge him out of the path of danger. It was a good plan. Except that the three large animals that went bounding majestically across the road materialized on Carl's side of the car. They seemed to come out of nowhere. Carl saw them just in time to brake into a sideways skid, so Ry got to see them, too, through Del's window, before the car spun completely backward and came to a halt. He turned and looked again through Carl's window in time to see the lovely animals bound away, unfazed.

Maybe they were fazed. Ry was fazed. Carl seemed unfazed as he turned the car again and drove on. He seemed to be aiming for the middle of the road now.

He was a really nice old man. He might be somebody's grandfather. Ry didn't want to hurt his feelings or be rude. But he also didn't want to die. He looked at Del. Del's face was on heightened alert, but he also appeared to be sticking with his look-down-the-road plan.

"What were they?" asked Ry.

"What were who?" asked Carl.

"Those animals that went across the road," said Ry. "They looked like deer, but different."

"Could have been," said Carl. "I can't say I was really paying attention."

"They were antelope," said Del. "Pronghorn antelope."

The car swerved abruptly back to the right and a couple of cars screamed by. The faces of the drivers of the cars turned toward Carl like sunflowers following the sun. Their mouths formed angry words. They made hand gestures.

"I don't know where everybody's going," said Carl, shaking his head. "Look around," he said, chuckling. "There's no place to go!"

Ry wished he could see better through the smeared windshield. He wished the dials on the dashboard worked. All of the needles rested, lifeless, at zero. Zero mph, zero rpm, zero gas. Zero mph sounded really good right now. Zero gas might be a good thing, if it were true. If they ran out of gas, they could get out of the barreling behemoth death trap. Dessicated insects had collected in the crevices both inside and outside the dials. Trying to get in, trying to get out.

Another dark, blurry shape seemed to be materializing

in the distance, growing in size and in loudness of rumbling. It pixelated ahead of them. In their lane. Which was legally its lane. It was time for a new plan. And a brilliantly simple idea formed in Ry's mind. He would say he was sick and he had to throw up. It was even sort of true. Once he got out of the car, he would not get back in. He would walk forever; he did not care now how far.

He was about to put his plan into action—his lips had parted to speak—when Del said, "Hey, Carl, can you pull over to the right up here? This is our stop."

"Hm?" said Carl. "Oh. All right. Of course. We'll just pull right over."

As he spoke, he somehow relocated his unfeeling, slippered foot onto the brake pedal and gradually slowed the car. He reflexively flipped on his turn signal, steered expertly into the narrow parking area in front of a long, low shedlike building, stopped neatly at the opening onto the porch. A competent driver had stepped forward on the runaway bus that was Carl, a cowboy jumped onto the wild pony and settled it down. A fragment of the real Carl, unfogged by time, had surfaced. Momentarily.

Ahead of them large, bright letters on a giant sign that even Carl's eyes could make out told them that this was CECILE'S TRADING POST. Underneath it said that Cecile's had GAS*SNACKS*AMMO*BAIT*SOUVENIRS*CRAFTS.

"Out looking for souvenirs, are you?" asked Carl.

"I need some postcards," said Del. "I want to write to my friends and tell them about my vacation." He was out of the car. Ry was right behind him.

"Good for you," said Carl. "Tell them all I said hello."

"Thanks for the lift," said Ry.

"Glad to help out," said Carl. He winked. "My good deed for the day."

He threw the car into reverse, cranked the steering wheel, and reared back in a tight arc. But before he could pull out, Del was over at the passenger side window again, his hands resting on the door.

"Listen," he said. "I noticed your muffler is dragging. I can hook it up so it doesn't drag till you can get somewhere, if you have a coat hanger in the car. Take me about two seconds."

"Oh, I don't have anything like that, I don't think," said Carl. Looking over his shoulder into the backseat.

"Let me just ask inside this place then," said Del. "They probably have something we can use. Can you hang on just a minute while I go in and see?"

"Well, all right," said Carl.

"I'll be right back," said Del. As he passed Ry, he said, "Go talk to him. Don't let him drive away."

Ry stepped uncertainly toward the car, his hands in his pockets.

"So . . . ," he said. He hadn't had a lot of practice at making conversation with old geezers. Except for his grandfather, but that was different. His grandfather still had all his marbles.

"So, what's in all those boxes back there?" he asked.

Carl looked over his shoulder again, then back at Ry.

"No idea," he said. "Looks like someone's moving, maybe."

"Aren't they yours?" asked Ry.

"Nope," said Carl. "I never saw them before today."

"How did they get in your car?" asked Ry.

"Oh, this isn't my car," said Carl. "I don't have a car. I used to have cars. I have had many, many a car in my time." He smiled, a sweet smile. A glimmer of—mischief?—seemed to pass through his eyes. Ry wondered if he had imagined it. He knew Del had only been inside for a couple of minutes, but it seemed like forever. He couldn't think of any more topics.

He was about to ask, Well, whose car is it then? when

hinges creaked behind him. He turned with relief to see Del come back outside with a coat hanger in his hand.

"Got one," said Del, holding it up. "This should do it."

But in the passing instant that the top half of Ry was turned toward Del, the lower half of Carl found a way to let his weight fall hard on the gas pedal. The Oldsmobile spun out of the dirt and clattered up onto the hard road, throwing up a choking curtain of dust into their faces. It roared off.

By the time they could see it again, the Oldsmobile was half a mile away.

"I hope he doesn't kill anyone," said Del.

"Should we report him? To the police or something?" asked Ry.

"I reported him to Cecile," said Del. "She said she would call. I guess we better go ask her to call again."

## (POST–CARL)

Later, when Del was putting the generator back into the Willys, Ry said, "So, how come twisting the wires together would be shoddy, but hooking up a muffler with a coat hanger isn't?"

"It is," said Del. "But that was an emergency. It was a desperate measure."

"Isn't it an emergency when your car dies in the middle of nowhere?" asked Ry.

"It could be," said Del. "If your life was in danger. Otherwise, it's just an interesting situation. You could even think of it as fun."

He had soldered the broken wire together over a small fire they built. Ry had helped lay the fire and he held things in place while Del soldered, but he had the feeling that Del would have managed just fine by himself.

The plan had been to walk to a town, find a mechanic to solder the wire, maybe get a ride back. But while they were at Cecile's, Del found this dinky little soldering tool in a jewelry-making kit. The kit was in the crafts section, a dusty pile of battered boxes. Del happened on it by luck, while Ry searched for food they could call breakfast.

It turned out to be a parallel-universe breakfast. A long shelf-life version; you didn't want to know how old any of it was. Just be like an astronaut and choke it down. He picked jerky, pickled eggs, potato chips, and orange soda. Corresponding to bacon, scrambled or fried, home fries, and juice.

It was not only the food that was of indeterminate age at Cecile's. Without even exploring very far, Ry found small American flags with the wrong number of stars, yellowing comic books with heroes he had never heard of, and music on cassette tapes. The cars in the postcards all looked like—well, Carl's or Del's, so he couldn't really draw any conclusions there. But the little girls and women were wearing dresses, an old-fashioned kind with big full skirts. Maybe it was more of an antique shop. He brushed past a spinning rack of brochures that illustrated a variety of ways of going to HELL in hand-drawn wavy letters, and found himself in a small section of actual groceries. Maybe this was a better idea. He picked up a box of Cheerios. The sell-by date stamped on the top was two years past. The contest deadline on the back of the box, likewise. Antique cereal. It might still be okay. According to legend, Twinkies lasted for seventeen years. Maybe Cheerios did, too.

He decided to go with the stuff up front. It was probably the faster-moving stuff. Relatively. He went back up to the counter. Del was already there, taking money from his wallet to pay for the food and—a jewelry kit?

"You don't by any chance have a cup of coffee you could spare?" he asked Cecile. Who was herself ageless, in a way. And preserved.

Her smile was lively.

"You bet," she said. She disappeared through a curtained doorway and returned with a Styrofoam cup of steaming brown toxins.

"Don't worry about it," she said when Del asked her how much.

"Do you need a lift?" she asked. "I can call someone."

Del said no thanks, and as they started their hike back toward the car, juggling the generator, the jewelry kit, "breakfast," and Del's coffee, Ry asked him why.

"No sense making someone go out of their way," said

Del. "We can probably get a ride with someone who's already going where we need to go."

And even as he spoke, he turned and raised his thumb, along with his coffee cup, at a passing tractor trailer. The trucker tootled at them and eased his rig to a halt a few dozen yards ahead.

"Don't worry," said Del as they trotted toward it. "Most people are nice."

"I'm not worried about 'nice,'" said Ry. "Carl was 'nice.'"

Del smiled his almost-smile.

"And most people are better drivers than Carl," he said.

Ry was worried, a little, about "nice." Maybe more than a little. Like five-eighths. But he didn't say so.

His inner voice issued warnings. He climbed up into the cab anyway. Why did he? Because sometimes it's hard to tell if your inner voice is wise, or if it's made out of your fears and your mother's fears and too many psycho-killer movies all balled up and clamoring. So he went along with the crowd outside of himself—Del and the sunny day and the shiny truck. It could have gone wrong, it could have been bad, but it turned out okay. The guy was just a guy. He knew how to drive. Before long they said, "Thanks" and climbed back down.

The Willys looked like home, though.

When they got there, they made the fire. Del soldered the wire and put the generator back into its place. They climbed in, the Willys started up, and off they went.

They had not been traveling long when, in the distance, a dot appeared. A dot with its headlights on, wavering from side to side, growing larger. Coming at them in their lane, skipping back over to the other. Boxy now, and whitish, way bigger than a bread box. A head, silvery, hanging out the window; a hand, too, reaching to adjust the outside mirror. Maybe for a better look at the other dot growing into a box behind it. That one had a flashing red light on top. It was catching up.

As soon as they knew the first car was Carl, Del eased off the road out into the dirt where it was safe. No sooner done than Carl whizzed by, close enough that they could see his eyes, and the delight and terror in them. He saw them, too, and maybe it was trying to recall who they were that made him lose what grasp he had of what he was doing. The big old car went zigzagging; it tipped up onto two tires, the two on the right. For a long half second, it could have come back down on four or tipped right over, either one. It went over. And over again. And lifted slightly once more, but fell back down with a whomp.

Light wisps of smoke rose from the folded hood as the cop car pulled off, a distance behind. Wisps thickened to plumes as the cop doors flew open. Del had backed up, turning, as if to head down there, too. But the cops jumped from their car and ran, and it was plain that they were the ones in a position to do anything.

The plumes of smoke inflated to clouds as the policemen tried to open the door but couldn't. One of them reached inside, lifted Carl from under his armpits, hauled him mightily through the open window. Carl's arms wrapped around the cop's shoulders in an embrace, like a child with his mother. The cop set him down on the ground, but when his legs crumpled and he started to sink so rapidly, both men were there, lifting him back up. Hurrying him away, they looked back over their shoulders. The thick smoke grew thicker and blacker; a dark geyser poured up into the clear air.

And then, like the striking of a match, there was flame that exploded into fire. The car was a torch. It was impossible to look away from a fire like that. Del and Ry and Carl and the policemen all watched it, transfixed.

When the flames gave way to smoke again and another flashing light–topped vehicle could be seen, the two burly cops led subdued, small Carl to their car. Del pulled quietly back on to the road. There was nothing he could tell the police that they wouldn't see for themselves immediately. The Willys headed east. They moved on. Everyone moved on, to whatever happened next.

Everyone thought about the fire, though, about what had happened and what could have happened. Del and Ry didn't say much for a while. Ry thought about Carl, all small and round and frightened. He thought about how he himself had been in that car, with Carl driving.

But there was a limit to how long he could think about all that. It got too deep. He had to rise to the surface.

"So," he said to Del brightly, "are you from around here, or are you just passing through?"

# NORTH DAKOTA

They stopped in a town in North Dakota for lunch and to get gas. It was late for lunch. The place was almost empty.

Ry was going to have a burger, but then he thought he should eat some vegetables, so he ordered a BLT. And a milkshake.

"At least he didn't get killed," he said. Meaning Carl, and Del got that. He had been thinking of Carl, too. And something else.

"How old is your grandfather?" he asked.

"I don't know," said Ry. "Seventy, something like that."

"Is he pretty healthy?" asked Del.

"He plays tennis," said Ry. "He skis. And water-skis."

"How about mentally?" asked Del. "Do you think he would ever wander off? Is he like Carl?"

"No," said Ry. "He's not like that. He's still all there. He's probably the smartest person in our family."

So, if he wasn't answering the phone, or returning Ry's calls, why wasn't he? It had to be something just weird and simple. As weird and as simple as how just saying the words "our family" made Ry wonder if he still had one. Where was everyone?

He was glad there was Del. Otherwise, he might be living under that bridge in New Pêche. In a cardboard box.

"You can imagine fifty million things," said Del, as if he had heard Ry's thoughts. "But only one thing happened. And most of the time, it's just a mix-up, not something bad. So you might as well not worry. Just go find out."

"I don't think I can help wondering," said Ry.

"That's why we're going there," said Del.

The waitress arrived with their food. It looked great. Like food for the gods.

"I didn't order a pickle," Del said to the waitress.

"Oh, we always put a pickle on," she said pleasantly.

"I don't like pickles," said Del. "I really don't even want it on the same plate as my food."

"Jeez," said Ry. "It's just a pickle. Here, I'll take it."

The waitress lifted her eyebrows and moved on.

"I can still smell it," said Del. "I really dislike the smell of vinegar." He said "vinegar" the same way he had said "shoddy." The same way you might say "cannibal." Ry thought he was overreacting a little.

Still, there was a stack of clean plates on a counter nearby, so he went and got one and brought it back. He transferred Del's sandwich and fries to the clean plate, saying, "My hands are clean. I just washed them." He set the used plate on the counter. Sitting back down, he said, "What about my pickle? Will it ruin your lunch if I have a pickle?"

"I don't know why you would want to," Del said. "But it's your life."

Ry ate both pickle spears. They were tart and crisp and succulent. The soft white bread was homemade. The bacon melted and crunched in his mouth. The tomato was ripe and tasty. The lettuce was just lettuce, but it did what it was supposed to do; it was green. The milkshake, chocolate, was cold and thick, yet not completely impossible to suck up through the straw. And there were fries. Fresh, warm, tender-crisp, and salty.

Ry was suffused with a sense of well-being.

Del said, "Let's just drive straight through."

"What?" said Ry. Because he had been immersed in

eating. By the time he finished saying it, he knew what Del had said; it had registered. Del opened the road atlas he had brought in with him. He flipped back and forth between pages marked with forefingers and thumbs. He had pulled out reading glasses, and they slipped down his beakish nose, making him appear older. Almost old. Or maybe that was because his cap was off, and with his head tilted down his scalp shone from beneath thinning hair.

"Might as well," he said. "See how far we can get, anyway. I think we can make it by morning. Then you can yell at your grandfather for not answering the phone."

He looked up at Ry. His grin was impish. Now he seemed younger again.

"Wasn't there stuff you wanted to do on the way?" asked Ry. "Errands?"

"Nothing that can't wait," said Del. "I can do it on my way back. Let's just go."

So they headed out across the rest of North Dakota. There was a lot of that left.

Not to mention all that Minnesota.

Not to mention all that Wisconsin.

# DOGS

## ROAD TALK

With lightning flashing in the distance, Ry said how he wanted to go home but that it wasn't exactly like home, just a house with their stuff in it.

"The dogs will make it feel better," he said. "And my grandfather. Assuming he's there."

After riding along for another half hour, he said, "I have my learner's permit. I could help drive if you want. I think."

For a while, their conversation was instructional. Del telling Ry what to do. For a while, Ry forgot about his predicament. He was absorbed in operating the Willys. It was a little different than a Focus wagon, though he had already started to learn how to drive with a stick. This stick came out of the dashboard. It was called Three on a Tree.

Del didn't like the kind of steering where you only had

to turn the steering wheel a little, so he had changed the gear ratio and exchanged the original steering wheel for one from some other old kind of car. It was huge. It was like steering a ship down the road. The road itself was straight. Once he got used to the driving, Ry's mind was able to meander around other topics at the same time.

"So, do you really have errands between Montana and Wisconsin?" he asked Del. Because looking around, he couldn't think what anyone would do here. No offense to North Dakota, but it was pretty subtle so far. There were a lot of green fields, with ponds and waterfowl, sometimes a bright yellow field. There were wide-open spaces and a lonely kind of green monotonous peacefulness that he knew his mother would really get off on. If she could go for a hike with the dogs, and if she could find a good cup of coffee. But he was still young and preferred some stimulation. Other human beings, for example. Other young human beings. Maybe groups of them, though even one or two would be a start.

"Not errands, exactly," said Del. "Just people I like to visit when I can."

"Where do they live?" asked Ry.

"I have a couple of friends in St. Paul," said Del. "And a friend down in San Juan that I might drop in on."

"San Juan?" said Ry. "In Puerto Rico? I wouldn't call that 'on the way.'"

"Just depends on how you look at it," said Del. "Once you leave home, anything can be on the way."

He told Ry about how, a long time ago, after he got out of the army, he decided to go around the world. He hitchhiked a lot, and washed dishes. Bought or found old bicycles, fixed them up, rode them around, and then left them behind for someone else. He bought a car once. An army surplus ambulance. In Australia. And then he decided to drive around the perimeter. Of Australia.

Del was not a talkative guy. Ry had to keep saying, "And then what happened?" and "Where did you go after that?"

"How did you decide where to go next?" asked Ry. "Did you have a sort of a plan?"

"My plan was to go from east to west," said Del. "But we would hear about someplace that sounded interesting, and we would go there."

"So you weren't by yourself?" asked Ry.

"Sometimes I was," said Del. "But you meet people."

Somewhere in the Australia part of the story, Del and Ry traded back and Del was driving again. It turned into a bedtime story in India, while some guy was trying to sell fake emeralds to Del and a friend he had met up with. Ry woke up in his sleeping bag in the back of the Jeep. He didn't remember how he had gotten there.

The vibration of the truck bed, the muffled rumble of the engine, the feel of the road bumping beneath told him they were still moving. Through the night. Somewhere in Minnesota or Wisconsin. Getting closer to the mystery he was trying to think of as home.

Del was talking, up in the front. As if he were talking to someone. And it came to Ry that this had happened before. He remembered, then, half waking on Del's couch, peering through barely parted eyelids as Del argued with himself, and how unsettled it made him feel. He tried to pay attention now, because he wasn't quite as tired this time. It was hard to hear. Rain pelted the roof, and the wipers were working.

"I've never been there," he heard Del say. "But I've heard it's pretty."

Maybe he was just talking to stay awake.

"Do you do much rafting?" Del asked.

Ry waited to hear how he would answer himself. Then was startled to hear a different voice, right behind his head, saying, "Oh, yeah, now and then."

"I'm more into biking," the voice said. It was a different person. Del must have picked up a hitchhiker.

Ry lay still, listening. He hoped the guy wasn't going to stay with them for the whole trip, like the ones Del picked up in Australia. He wanted to ride in the front. Although, theoretically, Ry's part in the trip was supposed to be done by morning anyway.

I guess it doesn't really matter, he said to himself as his eyes closed. He rose almost to consciousness again when he felt the brakes grabbing hold, heard the door open, the hitchhiker saying, "Thanks," Del saying, "Good luck." The door banged shut, then they were moving again. The rain was still pelting.

"It's not just a pickle," Del said into the rainy night. "It's the principle. I didn't order a pickle. I didn't want a pickle. So why do they bring me a pickle?"

Half an hour later, he added, "I shouldn't have to list all the things I don't want them to bring me."

Ry didn't hear him. He was dreaming about climbing the face of a cliff wearing flip-flops. Sometimes the flip-flops changed into Pumas. Or waterlogged hiking boots. When he had almost reached the top, he lost his footing (and his hand-ing) and went falling through the air. The funny thing was, he fell slowly. He could see everything on the cliffside with clarity. It all seemed very beautiful:

A bird watching him from its hollow. A stubborn flower growing out of a minute fissure. The rock itself, in layers of changing color.

He couldn't grab onto anything, but he didn't seem to be worried. He was pretty sure his dad was waiting at the bottom with the car.

"Was it fun?" his dad would say, looking up from his magazine.

"In a way," Ry would answer. "I mean, it wasn't life threatening."

~~~~~~~~~~

Everything was still, except for the light, peaceful snoring. The snoring emanated from the sleeping lump of Del, curling away into a question mark. Ry sat up and pushed the sleeping bag from his sweaty legs. It was already warm in their sauna, and stuffy. He pushed the flowered curtains apart a few inches and looked outside to see where they were.

He saw a parking lot. Empty, except for them, so it was still early. Beyond the parking lot was a small wasteland, and then what looked like a dealership for manufactured homes. Remnants of clouds hung low, but offered no clues about what location they overhung.

Trying to be quiet, Ry crawled over into the front seat and let himself out. As muggy as it was, the air felt fresher than it had inside. It felt a lot fresher than he felt himself. Just checking on that, he took a whiff. Holy crap. To put it politely.

The parking lot had an abandoned aspect. Weeds grew up verdantly through ruptures in the asphalt, where frost heaves had lifted it then let it collapse. Broken glass, gravel, and litter lay undisturbed on the rolling, buckled surface. A fallen light pole rested diagonally over the weathered paint lines marking out parking spots.

In the middle of it all was a shopping plaza. Or at least that's what it had been, once. It looked as if it might be a dead plaza now. Not completely dead—a couple of storefronts seemed to be toughing it out. There were lights on in the Laundromat, and the Something-or-other Diner. Ry squinted. It was the Good Deal Diner.

A small flock of cars huddled up close to it. Ry watched another car come in off the road, cross the parking lot, and join the flock. The car doors opened wide, people spilled out, the car doors banged shut, the people milled over and inside. Their chatter reached Ry as a cheerful murmur. He turned and looked the other way and up and down the road to see what else there was. Traffic was light. It was one of those roads at the edge of a town where fast food places and quick-lubes and discount furniture stores sprout up in the margins of the farm fields. A homey old farmhouse nestled in a clump of trees a ways back, pretending it was still in the countryside. Across the road was a Home Depot. It could be anywhere. Meaning, so could they.

Del was still snoring. He had driven most of the night. Ry decided to go to the diner and use the restroom and get some breakfast. He rolled down the window for ventilation, then gently clinked the door shut.

He tried to wash up a little in the restroom. He could

only go so far; there was just one sink and people kept coming in and out. The bruise on his brow was fading nicely, going yellow like a leaf in autumn, but not beautiful like that. The swelling was way down, the shape of his eye opening was almost normal. He checked his wallet, went out into the restaurant, and sat on a stool at the counter.

Breakfast and lunch menus were up on the wall, on black signs with white plastic letters and numbers that could be moved around by pushing them into horizontal grooves. Everything sounded great. Ry glanced at the breakfasts of his nearby fellow diners to see what looked good. It all looked good.

He ordered waffles. And an omelet. And sausage. As he waited, he let his thoughts wander. His gaze wandered, too, bouncing here and there. It bounced on a sticky circle on the counter where the syrup dispenser had been and stuck there for a few seconds. Followed the fly that also got stuck there, then licked his way free, like shoveling snow from around the tires of a car, and flew off in that drunk-driver fly way.

He half-listened to a loud conversation in a booth behind him about someone named Bob, who was a bum. Or not. There were two opinions. The people had that Wisconsin way of talking: "Baahhb" for "Bob," "waahh-ter" for "water."

He looked up at the lunch part of the menu on the wall. It listed everything you would expect. At the bottom, in quotation marks, the sign said, BEST BURGERS IN WAUPATONEKA. His eyes reached "Waupatoneka" and stopped dead in their tracks. Then looked out the window. Nothing looked familiar. But, then—

The waitress brought his food. She had noticed the funny-looking car out in the parking lot when she came in to work. She had seen Ry crawl out of it. She even happened to be looking out the window when he sniffed his armpit, and smiled to herself. She was aware of the amount of time he spent in the little restroom, and could tell by the wetness of Ry's hair around his face that he had been doing a little cleaning up. He was cute, even with the nasty-looking bruise on his eyebrow. He looked temporarily scruffy, but you could tell by his manner that he was a nice kid.

"Are you from around here?" she asked.

"Yeah," said Ry. "I live here." He was going to add, "I think," but that would have required explaining. It was way too long a story to tell to a waitress bringing you breakfast. Though she seemed kind, and he wouldn't have minded.

She was unconvinced anyway. Reflexively, they both

looked out the window at the Willys. Or where it had been. It wasn't there now. The waitress looked back at Ry. His face had changed.

The parking lot was empty everywhere Ry could see, except for the cars parked right out front. So, what was happening; did Del just leave? Wake up and drive away? Here's your town; you're on your own.

It seemed weird that he would go without saying good-bye, without saying anything at all. Although Ry himself had done that. He had crawled out of the Jeep and left without a word while Del was sleeping. But he thought Del would be sleeping for a long time. Del had driven all night.

So here he was in Waupatoneka, on his own. Okay. It wasn't a part of Waupatoneka he had seen before, that he could recall, but it couldn't be too far from his house. The town wasn't that huge.

He turned back to his breakfast and wondered why he had ordered so much food. He cut off a corner of waffle and dipped it in syrup. As he chewed, he looked back outside as if the Willys might magically reappear. It didn't. Even after chewing, the bit of waffle didn't want to go down his throat.

A man's form materialized outside the diner door, opened the door, and came inside. At first his face was neutral as he scanned through the faces in the booths, at the tables, and the counter. When Del's eyes found Ry, they lightened and he seemed relieved, and Ry felt foolish for freaking out. But what else should he have thought?

"I thought you might be in here," said Del, sitting down on the next stool, looking up at the menu, nodding yes when the waitress said, "Coffee?"

# DOGS

# KIND OF WEIRD

Finding Ry's house wasn't hard once they made their way from the scraggly it-could-be-anywhere zone to the old downtown. Ry knew his way from there. He had walked it a few times; a few lefts and a right and there it was.

His grandpa's car was parked in the driveway. Warm relief flowed through Ry. Quick on its heels came a colder, clammier wave of apprehension. He tried to shrug it off, but he couldn't, not quite.

The front door was locked, and so was the back. That was weird. Ry tried both doors, then rapped on them. He peered through the windows, but he couldn't see anything. Or hear anything. No footsteps, no TV, no barking dogs.

Then he noticed that the back door to the garage was

open. Not only unlocked, but open. Ajar. Just an inch or two. He stepped inside and paused for an instant while his eyes adjusted. There was the food and the water bowls for the dogs, alongside a giant open bag of dry chow.

Ry reached for the doorknob on the door that led from the garage into the kitchen. This one was unlocked. Lucky. He stepped up into the house. Del came in behind him. They both felt the insides of their noses curl up and shrivel somewhat.

The smell turned out to be coming from the coffee pot. The little orange light was on. Ry flicked off the switch and lifted the glass carafe from the warming plate. A thick, tarry substance in the final stages of coffee death was enameled to the bottom. The aroma was no longer of anything you would want to put inside your body. Ry turned and showed Del the pot.

"It was still on," he said. "You want some?"

"No, thanks," said Del. "I think I'll pass."

He came over and looked at it, though. It was only nine o'clock in the morning. They both knew that it took more than a few hours to cook a slab of solid coffee like that. It wasn't from today. Maybe not even yesterday.

"Let's just take a look through the house," Del said, "and make sure everything's okay."

So Ry led Del up the stairs and into the hall. When they reached a doorway, he stepped back and held out his hand as if in courtesy, "After you." If everything was not okay, he didn't want to find out first.

His parents' room was disheveled, but they had disheveled it themselves, packing for their trip before they finished unpacking from the move. The covers had been pulled up on the bed, and a lone photograph had made it up onto the wall. The rest of it was a free-form jumble. Ry saw the layers of clothing draped over the back of his mother's chair and knew that she had changed her clothes at least three times, just to go to the airport.

Ry's room was just as he had left it, too. He didn't know anyone in this town yet, so there had been plenty of time to set his room up the way he wanted it. The decorating style he preferred was somewhere between Extreme Lived-in and Total Pit. *Lair* was how he thought of it. So at first glance it was as chaotic as his parents' room. Maybe more so. He had a lot more stuff on the walls than they did, and more things plugged in. He would have liked to just stay in there for a while and soak up the ambience, but Del moved on, and Ry made himself follow.

They went into the small spare bedroom where his

grandfather had set up camp. This room was orderly. The bed was made. An open book waited facedown on top of the clock radio on the nightstand. Several shirts hung in the open closet, along with a pair of blue jeans and a pair of khaki trousers, neatly folded in half on the hangers. A pair of moccasins had been dropped onto the floor.

The bathroom was tidy and clean. Almost too tidy and clean. It was as sparkly and shiny as a bathroom in a hotel.

"I wonder where his toothbrush is," said Del, "and his razor."

They went back into the bedroom and looked around, opened the drawers in the dresser. They saw socks and underwear, but no toothbrush, no razor or anything like that.

"That's kind of weird," said Ry. "His car is here."

They went back downstairs and Ry led the way to the basement. Then up again and out onto the back porch. They went out into the yard and walked around. They looked inside the garage. Nothing seemed odd or amiss, except that no one was there. No dead bodies, but also no grandpas. No dogs. Not sure what else to do, they headed back inside.

A small hill of mail had fallen to the floor from the

slot in the front door. A couple of days' worth, maybe. Ry gathered it up and riffled through coupon flyers addressed to Occupant, a magazine, and some envelopes with the yellow forwarding stickers, something from the electric company. He set it all on the coffee table and sank into his dad's favorite chair. He closed his eyes. He considered keeping them closed until everything had turned out okay. Then he opened them and looked around at the familiar furniture of his life that had moved into this house and taken up residence. He was glad to see it all—the lamps, the knickknacks, the throw pillows. The steadfast couch welcomed him like a childhood friend.

It seemed for a time as if he might sit in the chair all day, or forever. But then, in a surprise move, his limbs assembled themselves and propelled him to the answering machine, on the desk in the alcove off the front hallway. It was blinking. The number of messages it wanted to deliver was ten. Ry found a piece of paper and a pen, and pushed the button.

# ANYWAY, LISTEN

The first three messages were his own. Maybe the fourth, too; it was a hang-up call.

The next one was from Ry's parents. His mother said that they had climbed a volcano, a mostly but not completely dead one. *Dormant*, that was the word. It had jungles growing all over it. And monkeys. Greenish monkeys. She wasn't sure if that was their natural fur color or if they were moldy. She had called to tell Lloyd that they were having a really nice time, but they had lost their cell phone somewhere along the way. If he needed to reach them, he should just check the itinerary for where they were going to be and leave a message there.

The message after that was from a doctor's office. A woman's voice said that she was following up on Mr. Farley's visit to the emergency room.

Would he please call this number and let her know how he was doing?

Ry scribbled down the number.

The emergency room? His grandpa?

The machine beeped, the number changed from five to four, and his mother's voice was talking again. As if to someone next to her, she said, "It is the right number; it has Ry's voice on it."

And, into the phone again, "Dad, we just wanted to let you know we're not where we're supposed to be right now. In case you tried to call us there. We are— (aside again) where are we? Saint who? (and back into the phone) We are on Saint Anomie. Anomalie. Amalie. Ennui. Henri. Something like that. It's a French name, it starts with an 'ah.' Annalee, maybe. They speak with a strong accent. It's beautiful, but I have trouble making out some things. And I hate to keep asking.

"Anyway. We had an eventful day today. We got blown off course. We were in some fairly strong winds, but we were doing all right until the mast snapped in half. Like a toothpick. The main one, with the biggest sail. I won't go into all the details, I didn't even know what was going on half the time, but let me tell you, I was glad to get to this little island, whatever it's called.

"So, let me give you the number here." There was some fumbling and some muffled conversation, then his mother repeated a phone number someone was giving her. "We'll stay here tonight and then try to find another boat tomorrow. With a better mast. But everything's fine; all's well that ends well. Skip twisted his ankle when he jumped off the boat, but we have it wrapped up really nicely in an Ace bandage and he can walk on it. Sort of.

"And now we're going to go find some beverages with umbrellas in them. At least, that's what I want. Bye for now."

*Click. Beep.*

Number eight was a hang-up call.

Now Ry heard his grandfather's voice.

"Listen," his grandfather said. "This is Lloyd. I hate to bother you, I really do. I'm sure you have a lot going on. The thing is—I don't know where the hell I am. I thought you might be able to tell me. Did I have any travel plans that you know of?"

There was a pause. A long pause. Then his grandfather said, "Oh, no!" Softly, as if taken by surprise. There was a crashing sound, followed by a harsh groan, as if of pain. And then a click.

A beep. Ry's dad spoke this time.

"Lloyd? Are you there? Are you okay? We're concerned that you're not answering the phone. I suppose we're just missing you, or maybe you don't have your hearing aid turned on. We'll keep trying.

"Anyway, listen, we've had another little glitch. We got the new boat, and we sailed today to a little island called Saint Jude's. All that is fine. But we went swimming at this beautiful beach that we thought was totally deserted. Only apparently it wasn't, because while we were in the water, everything we left on the beach disappeared. Passports, credit cards, even our beach towels.

"Fortunately, we have clothes on the boat and some cash that we tucked away. But we will be here for a few days, anyway, waiting for our stuff. Tomorrow is some kind of a holiday, and I guess nobody does anything over the weekend, unless maybe your life is in danger.

"By Monday we should have everything we need. I'm not sure where we'll go then; we're a little up in the air about that. We're just going to bunk on the boat; we don't have a number where you can reach us right now. We'll call again as soon as we know more.

"Okay. I guess that's it. Bye for now. Answer the phone next time, okay?"

The familiar voices floated in the air, then they were gone. The machine announced the End of Messages. Ry had pulled the chair out to sit down at the desk while the messages played and, for a moment, he sat there without moving. He wanted to hear the voices again, but he wanted them to say different things. Or to be coming out of the actual people, who would be standing there beside him.

# THE MYSTERY OF RY'S GRANDPA

It wasn't like a soap opera, where the person has amnesia and doesn't remember who he is. Lloyd knew exactly who he was. The part of his brain that had been bruised and jumbled was the part where more recent information was processed. The waiting room of his brain, the lobby, where information paced back and forth while it waited to find out what room it would be housed in. Sometimes the information went around a corner, and he couldn't locate it. Then it would appear again. Sometimes the information just disappeared and never came back.

This made it hard to watch television. He could watch game shows, where they asked for trivia from the past. But the programs that required you to keep track of what had happened just before the commercials? No. Mostly not. His hand went to a bump on his head. It felt tender.

He did not know how he had come to be in this hotel room.

Looking for clues in his wallet, Lloyd found a piece of index card cut down to fit inside one of the slots. Three phone numbers were written there, in his own handwriting, next to the names of his daughter, her husband, and his grandson. He had noted that two of the numbers were cell phone numbers.

There was a telephone in the room. Lloyd called all three numbers. No one answered. "Leave a message," they all said. Well, what good would that do? What if he wasn't here anymore when they called back? He decided to leave a message anyway, at the number that wasn't a cell phone. As he spoke, he pushed open the drapes and looked out the window. For Pete's sake, he thought. I'm a reasonably intelligent person. I know my address and I have credit cards; I'm sure I can get home. Then he would go see his doctor and figure it out.

He had the feeling he had already been to a doctor, but it was a blurry feeling. There was a blind spot in his thinking that kept moving around. But he thought he could work around it. He would just write things down as he figured them out. A notepad and a pen sat on the desk by the phone, and Lloyd picked them up.

He still held the phone to his ear, but he stopped speaking as he studied the scene outside. The license plates were a different color. What state was he in? Down on the quiet morning sidewalks, a movement caught his eye.

Two dogs, a reddish one and a black one, nosed along. They weren't accompanied by a human, which seemed odd on a city street. The black one rose up on its hind legs, rested its front paws on the lip of an overflowing trash can, and retrieved a wad of paper. Something fell from the paper when the dog shook its head, and both dogs snarfed it up.

Two dogs. A reddish and a black one.

"Oh, no!" he said softly. He was supposed to—

The two dogs trotted into an alley in the middle of the block and out of sight. Lloyd spun around so quickly that he went off balance, which didn't help the workings of his brain any. It was injured and susceptible, in the way that when you bite your tongue once, it seems to swell and then you chomp on the same spot over and over. Flailing to steady himself, he dropped the phone and knocked into the lamp with his elbow, his funny bone. The lamp crashed to the floor, and Lloyd let out a load groan of frustration and funny bone pain.

He replaced the receiver and righted the lamp. He

scrawled "dogs!" on the notepad and slipped it into his pocket, along with the pen. Then he hurried from the room, found the staircase, descended three floors worth of worn blue-carpeted steps and exited the building.

His eyes fell on the trash can and the fast food wrappers. A light summer breeze sent the crumpled paper skittering into the alley where the two dogs had disappeared, and Lloyd followed, too. The dogs weren't there anymore, but maybe he would be able to see them from the other end.

That street was a big street, and busy. Cars and trucks fumed in both directions, inching along, then shooting forward without mercy. There weren't a lot of people on the sidewalks, but the ones who were there meant business. The air was full of diesel exhaust, the sound of truck brakes, and the not-too-distant *peep-peep-peep* of something backing up. A motorcycle revved its engine. Pigeons stepped by, unconcerned. Their iridescent feathers were magnificent in the sunlight that fell straight down between the buildings. It was an east-west street.

Lloyd pulled the notepad from his pocket—"dogs." Right. He was looking for the dogs. He looked to his left, but saw no dogs. To his right, no dogs. He took out the pen and added, "Peg red, Olie black." That had popped into his head.

Across the street was a square green park. A vendor was setting up his hot dogs, buns, and condiments on a silvery cart. Beyond that, the park had a pond, with ducks. And there, watching the ducks, were the two dogs. Lloyd hurried to the corner and pushed the Walk button. His view of the pond was now blocked by bushes. When the light changed, he walked briskly across the street and into the park. Once there he saw the dogs leaving through an opening in the bushes on the far side.

"Peg!" he shouted. "Olie!" The dogs continued on their way. They made a right turn and then vanished. Lloyd hastened through the park in hot pursuit. The two dogs, who were not Peg and Olie, found their way to their own doorstep. By the time Lloyd walked past the tall narrow house in a row of many such houses, the dogs were having kibble and water in their kitchen.

Lloyd walked up and down the strange streets, looking for them. He could not recall how he had misplaced them in the first place. He was not familiar with this town. A map might help. If he could remember where he was supposed to go.

He felt he was on the verge of remembering all of it.

He came upon a restaurant with tables set up outside on a patio and decided to sit down there and think. He ordered coffee and a pastry. The license plates on the cars, he observed, were mostly Illinois plates. What the hell am I doing in Illinois? Lloyd wondered. The face of a woman flashed through his mind. He had met a beautiful woman. She had helped him in some way. When the waitress left the check, he reached for his wallet, only to find that it wasn't there. He stood up and checked all of his pockets. Twice. He had the notepad and the pen, and some loose change. No wallet. No cash. No credit cards. No phone numbers.

Lloyd smiled at the waitress as she refilled his cup and thanked her. Then he did something completely un-Lloydlike. He left his pocket change on the table—it wasn't enough, but it was all he had—and walked out on his check. He didn't look back. Feeling like a criminal, a fugitive, or at least a creep, he turned a corner at the first opportunity.

As Lloyd walked along, a car pulled up alongside him and kept pace with him. He was afraid to look at it directly, but he could see it from the corner of his eye. This was a seedier part of town, no sidewalk cafes or parks with ponds here. No houses, even. He glanced to his right into a derelict storefront. The display windows offered party supplies from some previous decade, one he hadn't paid attention to. The dirty windows reflected the image of the car behind him and he tried to see who might be inside, but that part of the reflection was blocked by his own image. In a burst of bravado, he turned and looked into the car. And wondered, calmly enough, if he might be hallucinating. Because there were two of them in there.

# WHEN THE RUG
# IS PULLED OUT—
# THE EARTH, TOO—
# YOU HAVE TO MOVE
# YOUR FEET TO KEEP FROM FALLING

Ry went to find Del. Maybe if he listened to the messages along with someone else, they would fall into place. Then he could laugh at himself for not getting it. He was willing to laugh at himself. He wanted to. The two of them listened, intently and carefully.

His mother's voice took up the most space, time-wise and chatteriness-wise, and it sounded like a lot of stuff had happened to them down there, but it was the two other messages, the ones about his grandfather, that pulled the rug out, the earth out from under Ry.

Del wanted to listen again, so they did. For the third time, Ry listened to his grandfather speak, heard his soft "Oh, no," the crash, then the groan. He looked at Del, still hoping for that simple, obvious explanation. Del seemed thoughtful.

"Let's call that doctor's office," said Del. "And find out why your grandfather was there."

So Ry did. At first the woman who answered the phone didn't want to tell him anything. She couldn't release confidential information. Then he explained that his grandfather was missing; maybe he had been hurt. When he said this, he was just trying to say something dramatic enough to make her tell him what he wanted to know. But when she transferred the phone call to the doctor and Ry said it again, he realized he was just telling the truth, and he felt afraid, for his grandpa and for himself.

"Excuse me," he said to the doctor, "can you hold on one second?" And he passed the phone to Del. And the pad of paper and the pen.

In the hours that followed, Ry and Del spoke with the neighbors, and then the police. Ry wanted to talk to Betty, the friendly lady from next door, but the neighbor in the house just beyond said Betty had gone to her high school reunion and would be gone for a few days. No one else seemed to know anything, though a couple of people said they had seen Lloyd walking the dogs, and that he had waved or nodded or said "hello" and seemed like a nice man.

One person had seen him walk with the dogs into the woods at the end of the street, and so the two officers headed down to take a look. Ry and Del went along. They walked the path that made a loop, and they walked it a number of times. Ry tried to think like a CSI person, but he wasn't sure what to look for. Dead bodies, right, but aside from that. Bits of torn fabric? Blood? A place where the underbrush had been trampled, a freshly dug mound of earth? The air was warm and thick and heavy. Nothing tried to move in it but the four of them, walking in slow circles, and a couple of birds and squirrels. The only other movement was plant growth. That was happening almost perceptibly.

When they returned to the house, the police went over the information Ry had given them. He also gave them a photo, from the refrigerator, of his grandfather at a birthday party. They said Ry should call right away if he heard anything, anything at all. And then they were gone.

Del asked if it might be okay for him to take a quick shower.

"I think it might clear my head," he said. "Plus, it's been a couple of days."

Alone, Ry wandered down off the porch and around

the house again. In the backyard he looked behind the shed that looked like a miniature barn, where the lawn mower, rakes, shovels, and things like that were kept. A circle of red plastic caught his eye. He waded into the weeds to see what it was.

He found the handheld part of a retractable dog leash. The retracting part, the strap itself was stuck in a split in a fallen log, then wrapped and tangled around a sapling or two before coming to a chewed-off end. The wrapping and chewing looked recent. He called out to Peg and Olie and walked deeper into the new-growth woods, calling as he went. He wanted his dogs. He wanted to hear some thrashing and panting as they came bounding toward him. He wanted them to practically knock him down when they jumped on him and slobbered all over his face. He called out over and over.

Back inside, Ry found himself standing in front of the refrigerator with the door open. His mother had left meals in the freezer for his grandfather, and a couple of the plastic containers were left half full in the fridge. He sniffed it, then nuked it and asked Del if he wanted some.

"Help yourself," Ry said. "There's more stuff in there." He was eating meat loaf. He wondered what would happen next. Like, right after he finished eating the meat loaf. Would Del leave now? Would Ry just stay here in this house by himself, while his grandfather was who knows where? There was food in the freezer. He could do it, just sit here and wait.

"I feel like my mom and my dad need to know," he said. "About my grandpa. It seems like they should be here. In case—well, in case anything. It could be something bad. And then I think they would want to be here. I mean, he's my mom's dad."

"I think you're right," said Del. "It would be a good idea to let them know what's going on."

"But I can't call them," said Ry. "And I don't think they're planning to call here again, for a while." He took a bite and chewed. Swallowed. It was like swallowing a bird's nest. The kind made with lots of mud. That's how it felt in his throat. He drank some milk. "And what if they call and I miss it, like I'm in the shower or something, and they go off to some other place where I can't call them?"

He honestly did not know what to do. He was thinking, maybe, the police here could call the police there. He didn't know what kind of emergency you had to have to do that.

"We know where they are," said Del. "Maybe we should just go find them." Like this was no big deal. Like it was the most obvious thing.

"Yeah, right," said Ry. "We'll just drive down there quick-a-minute."

Del's face did its trick where without actually moving any of its parts, you could tell he was smiling. You could tell he was amused. If you want to see how this is done, watch an old Clint Eastwood movie. *The Good, the Bad and the Ugly*, for example.

"That wouldn't really be as big a deal as you think it would," said Del. "I know a guy in Florida who could fly us to San Juan. And I know someone there who has a boat. We could get there pretty quickly."

"And you were thinking of going there anyway, right?" said Ry.

"My friend Yulia is the person in San Juan," said Del. "I haven't seen her in a while. I wouldn't mind going."

Yulia, thought Ry. Why do I know that name?

"I think maybe I need to take a shower now," said Ry. "I think my head needs clearing, too."

While he is doing so, a tribute to showers: They are amazing. You could call them "transformers." Especially if it's been a couple/few days. You feel like a different person afterward, a person who is ready. A person who can take it on. Deal with it. Whatever it might be. This fades over time, but for at least half an hour, everything is within the realm of possibility. For this reason, it may or may not be a good time to make decisions. If you decide to do something big right after a shower, maybe you should wait an hour. Count to 216,000, then decide. I don't know. I'm just saying.

"I hate to ruin their vacation," Ry said when he came downstairs. "They were pretty excited about it. They planned it for a long time."

"It doesn't sound like it's actually going that great," observed Del.

And so, in ten sentences or less (don't count; it's an expression), in the wink of an eye, from zero to sixty, Ry went from "Yeah, right," to throwing some clothes in a backpack and grabbing the money from his secret place.

They left notes. They asked a couple of the neighbors to watch for the grandpa and the dogs. They left the back garage door propped open, with the food and the water in there, for the dogs. They called the Humane Society. They left the kitchen door unlocked, in case Lloyd found his way home, too.

It seemed to Ry that they were being incredibly thorough and responsible. Covering all the bases. And then they got back into the Willys, to drive to the third sandpile on the left, on the Island of the Saint of Lost Causes, an emerald dot in the azure of the Caribbean Sea. The time was just a little past six, CDT. Waupatoneka slipped away from them like a twig dropped into a stream. Or a boot . . . into a river.

# PART THREE

PART THREE

# THE GOOD,
# THE BAD,
# AND THE ROTTEN

In the middle of Indiana, in the middle of the night, Del and Ry paid a social call. Ry thought it was late to be showing up at someone's house, but Del said it was only a few minutes from the freeway and he wouldn't feel right if he drove past without at least saying "hello." He said they wouldn't stop if the lights weren't on. So they rolled down the exit ramp, then crept through dark streets that were still, except for a flash of commotion and light spilling from a tavern door as it opened and shut. They pulled up in front of a little house barely visible behind the overgrown bushes and towering evergreens that filled the yard. A twinkle of lamplight made its way through the foliage, so they made their way up the short broken sidewalk, toward it.

The woman who answered the door was surprised

but happy to see them, or at least Del. She was friendly and welcoming to Ry, too, in his role as friend of Del. Her name was Sharon, and she told them to come in, come in!

"Can I get you a beer?" she asked Del. "Or do you want coffee? Are you going to drive through the night?"

Del said they were, but that one beer would be nice. Sharon looked at Ry and said she had some apple juice, would that be okay? Ry said, "Sure." She returned with bottles of beer for Del and for herself and two tiny child-sized juice boxes for Ry.

"Sorry," she said. "Life with a toddler. I have lots more in the fridge. Help yourself to as many as you want." Then, "So, what's the deal?" she asked Del. She curled up in a frayed armchair and folded her legs beneath her. "Where are you off to? What's the adventure?"

Del said they were driving to the Caribbean to find Ry's parents.

"Ha!" said Sharon. "Where are they?"

"We're not one hundred percent sure," said Del. "But how hard can it be? They're pretty small islands."

Sharon laughed again. Longer. With more *ha*'s. The way she laughed made Ry want to know how to say things to make her laugh again. She laughed as if Del had just said the funniest thing she had ever heard.

"There's a lot of water in between those little islands, though," said Sharon. "What're you gonna do about that?"

"I'm pretty sure we can borrow a boat," said Del. "Yulia's in San Juan."

"Ah, yes, Yulia," said Sharon. "And you will get to San Juan how?"

"I have a friend who lives south of Miami," said Del, "who has a plane."

"Couldn't we go on a boat to San Juan, too?" asked Ry.

"A plane is a lot faster," said Del. "Besides, I don't know anybody with a boat until San Juan. Do you?"

"Is it a really small plane?" asked Ry.

"About as small as a plane can be without being a toy," said Del. "He made it himself."

Sharon laughed. Her laugh was as good as before, but Ry didn't know if he was willing to go up in a homemade airplane over vast expanses of deep water just to hear someone laugh a beautiful laugh. Was he willing to do it to find his mother and father, though?

It might depend on how vast and deep the expanses of water were. Like, if they could see the island they were aiming for from where they started, he would do it. He had to admit that his geography was fuzzy. He had a general idea that all those islands were off the coast of

Florida, but that was about it. His brain did a search and came up with the words *Bermuda Triangle*, in bold type. Also *Pirates of the* . . .

Just then a small child in pajamas entered the room rubbing its eyes. It took one look at Ry and Del and began to bawl. Sharon held out her arms and the child ran to her and climbed into her lap, then turned and glared at them. Balefully.

"This is Miles," said Sharon. "Miles, this is Del and Ray."

"Ry," said Ry.

"Ry," repeated Sharon.

"Hi, Miles," said Del. "We've met, but you probably don't remember."

Ry waved and smiled. Miles glared.

"You should go home now," Miles said.

"We will," said Del. "Pretty soon."

"Now," said Miles. Ry was willing. Miles was looking like he could be a pain in the butt.

"What do you want me to do?" Del asked. "Stand on my head?"

Miles eyed Del warily, then nodded.

"All right," said Del. The next instant he was standing on his head in the middle of the floor. "Is that better?" he asked Miles. "Do you want to try to knock me over?"

Miles flew from his mother's lap to give Del a push. Del obligingly curled down onto the floor, flat on his back.

"Wow," he said. "You're pretty strong."

Miles was smiling now. Sharon was smiling. Even Ry was smiling. Del knew other toddler-pleasing tricks, too. He knew airplane, horsey, upside-down walking, swing the kid in a circle, steal my thumb, steal your nose, and many others. Sharon settled gratefully, gracefully, into her chair. Del only had to ask her a brief question and her talking would flow forth as a babbling brook. Before long, Ry was only half listening. He sipped from his tiny juice boxes and surveyed the room. Even he could tell it was a piece-of-crap house, but Sharon had made it homey. There were colorful pillows and curtains and a vase with flowers, like one of those magazine ads where they display bright new products in a ruin and it looks kind of cool.

Now Del and Sharon were talking about someone they both knew. At least Sharon was. She was a talker, once she got started. A yakker, really. Del was not a big talker. He reminded Ry sometimes of a detective in an old movie, one of those guys of few words. Ry half expected Del to say things like "I just might do that, ma'am," or "I wouldn't put it that way, miss."

A cat appeared on the scene, a cat of the large black variety, with fur as long as a llama's. It had the face of a cat who is easily offended, a cat who is pretty sure it won't like you. A smashed-face, tight-lipped cat.

Ry dangled his fingers in a welcoming gesture of friendship. The cat glared with yellow eyes. Maybe he was sitting in its chair. He scooched over and scratched the surface of the chair lightly, in a let's-share gesture. The cat stalked over and teleported itself into the geographical center of the space Ry had made for it.

Feeling he was making progress, Ry held his hand a few inches from the cat's face, so it could smell him and see what a great guy he was. The cat's head leaned forward as if that's what it meant to do, then it opened its tight lips and sank its pointy teeth into Ry's flesh. CraOWap!

Only for a second. Then it was sitting there innocently, a puddle of black hair with malevolent eyes. Some cats are just like that. Maybe it was one of those rescue cats that had trouble trusting people.

Ry decided he would like another juice box or two. Through hand signals (he held up the juice boxes, Sharon pointed), he indicated his plan and went into the kitchen.

He found the light switch in the traditional location, spotted the fridge, and headed out across the linoleum. But as he passed the sink, the last remaining molecular bonds holding the rotting wooden strands of subfloor together gave way. His foot and most of his leg went through the floor, and he found himself suddenly sitting. Where he landed felt spongy, too, and he leaned back onto his hands, trying to spread his weight as if he were on thin ice. The empty juice boxes had leaped from his hands and skidded across the floor.

The crack of the floor giving way and the thump when his butt made contact were surprisingly gentle sounds. He let out a yelp, though, as he sank, and the conversation stopped in the other room.

"Everything okay?" Sharon called out. Ry didn't answer right away. He was too busy absorbing the impact of what had just happened. A tumbling of footsteps came his way. The footsteps reached the threshold and came to a stop. He did not want to turn and look over his shoulder at the three faces he knew were positioned in the doorway.

Behind him Miles's voice said, "Uh-oh."

Sharon's voice said, "Oh, shit." It sounded almost pleasant when she said it.

Del's old western cowboy voice said, "I reckon your sink is leaking, ma'am." Or his detective voice said, "How long has your sink been leaking, miss?" Or, he just said, "Is there a leak under your sink?" But it sounded like the other two.

Ry turned his head toward them.

"I'm sorry," he said. "All I did was walk across the room."

Del grabbed him under the armpits and pulled. Sharon helped from the other side to guide his foot and leg back up through the hole. They moved around the hole in a circle, bouncing gingerly to find out how far-reaching was the rottenness of the subfloor.

"I noticed it was soft in spots," said Sharon. "But I didn't know it was that bad."

"Do you have any tools?" asked Del. He kneeled down and wiggled a piece of wood. It broke off in his hand like a stale graham cracker.

"I'll call someone," said Sharon. "Tomorrow. First thing."

"Do you have any wood?" asked Del. He leaned out and reached across the hole to open the cabinet under the sink. The floor of the cabinet had warped into a rippling landscape of rolling hills. Tilting villages of buckets and cleaning products nestled in the valleys. A drop of water fell from a joint in the pipe to a small puddle below it. A lake in the tilting village.

"I don't suppose you have a wrench?" asked Del.

"Actually, I probably do," said Sharon. "Jerry was going to fix it before I told him to get lost. He left everything here. I was going to try to figure it out myself. I just haven't had time."

It was midnight. An owl hooted beyond the open window as Del laid a couple of two-by-fours across the hole to kneel on. Crickets chirped in their sleep as he and Ry moved all the cleaning junk out of the cabinet into a corner of the kitchen. Sharon led Miles away to put him back to bed.

Del fixed the leak first. It wasn't that hard to do, and he explained it to Ry as he went along. He had Ry use the wrench so he would know how it should feel. Then he scored the linoleum with a utility knife outside the rottenness and had Ry start to yank it up inside that boundary, while he used a saber saw to cut away the warped floor of the cabinet. With the saw, Del cut the subfloor along the edge of the linoleum and, together, they ripped that up, too. It was mesmerizing and satisfying work to rip up the nasty stuff and toss it onto the growing pile. Ry almost hated to stop to use the bathroom, but he had to, so he hurried off.

"I'll be right back," he told Del. He wasn't sure where the bathroom was, but the house was tiny; it couldn't be hard to find. On his way there, he looked into a softly lit room and stopped. Miles and Sharon were fast asleep. Miles was under the covers, Sharon was outside them, curled around her child. A picture book lay open, facedown, a little away from them.

Ry felt the nobility of what he and Del were doing for this mother and her child. It was a new and interesting feeling, and he thought he would like to feel it some more. He tiptoed into the room. He looked around for a blanket or something that he could put over Sharon. Everything seemed to be small, or plastic, or small and plastic. Then he spotted a rumpled heap of fabric underneath some smallish plastic items.

He made his way over to it, picking out stepping stones of uncluttered clearings of carpet. Lifting the fabric up and letting it fall to its still-rumpled full size, he saw that it was a superhero cape, with a hood. The hood had pointy ears; it was a Batman cape. The cape was fuzzy; that was nice. He tiptoed over to the bed and prepared to drape the cape over the sleeping Sharon. She turned over onto her back and said, "Well, if that's how you feel about it."

Ry froze in his tracks. He glanced toward the doorway and considered bolting, then back at Sharon. Her eyes were still closed. She crossed her bare arms across her chest and drew up her knees, putting one bare foot over the other. Ry lay the cape over her, covering as much of her as he could. He had to choose between bare arms and bare feet. He chose arms because there was more square footage of them. Then he reached under the lampshade and turned out the lamp.

With only a dim path of light from the living room, finding open places on the carpet to step on was harder. He didn't want to break or crunch anything. He moved across the floor like a spastic flamingo, one foot always hiked up under him while he reconnoitered for the next landing.

As it was a small room, this only took three steps, but it seemed like a long time. With one more step before he could leap into the hall, he reached down, balancing carefully, to push aside a stuffed animal blocking his way. He hadn't noticed it coming in. His eyes were adjusting to the dim light, and as he reached down he saw the thing lift its head, observe his approaching hand, rise to its feet, and pad silently out of the room. Not before tossing him a quick glare with its faintly visible yellow-green eyes. It was the hostile wretched cat.

Ry jerked his hand back in surprise as the dark, evil blob moved away. His own sudden movement threw off his balance. He teetered and flapped his arms. The foot that was in the air lunged toward the toy-free zone of the hallway, landing with only a mild thump, but he was in the splits now and as both hands went to the floor to keep him from tipping over, one of them found something wet and viscous. He did not want to think about what it might be. He paused there, listening to the sawing and tapping coming from the kitchen and the quiet breathing of Sharon and Miles behind him.

He could not stay there for long, and as he worked his way back to a standing position, the words *pulled groin* presented themselves in his mind. The effort not to cry out caused his eyebrows to lift several inches and stretched his mouth into a cornucopia of anguished shapes. He found the bathroom. The stuff he had put his hand into was PB&J. Not so horrible. He washed it off, glancing up at his face in the mirror. Not too bad, compared to before. The eye shape was normal. Just a bruise, now.

Back in the kitchen, he knelt down to help Del. *Ow,*

he said silently, to himself. Then, despite all his noble, mighty efforts, there was Sharon, blinking, the Batman cape pulled around her shoulders.

"Oh my God, Del," she said. "What are you doing?" Her face had a stunned expression to it, which made Ry view the scene in a new way. She was probably thinking that a couple of hours ago she had a kitchen floor, albeit one with a soft spot, and now she had a gaping hole. A huge gaping hole. That would be dismaying. He could see her point of view. Plus the pieces of what used to be her floor were piled in a trashy heap on the shores, the rim of the crater.

"The leak is fixed," Del said calmly.

"You need to stop now," said Sharon.

"I can't stop," said Del. "I'm not finished. It wouldn't be right."

"What do I have to do to get you to stop?" asked Sharon. She put her hands on her hips.

"I guess you could call the police," said Del.

"Maybe I will," said Sharon. She folded her arms across her chest.

"Tell them someone is fixing your rotten floor against your will," said Del. Ry could tell he was enjoying himself. He kept his features still, but his eyes were twinkling.

Sharon didn't know what to say next. She let her hands drop to her sides.

"You should go to bed," said Del.

"How can I sleep with all this racket?" asked Sharon. Hands simulating racket.

"Shut the door," said Del. "I'll hammer as quietly as I can."

"You're not going to stop, are you?" she said. It wasn't a question. One hand returned to her hip. The other rested against the doorjamb.

"No," said Del. "Not yet."

She threw up her hands and walked away. A door closed. Another door closed. Ry and Del looked at each other. Del's smile broke out from inside into the open, full force.

"It's just dangerous to have a hole in the floor, especially with a little kid," he said. By way of explanation.

"I can't believe I put my foot through someone's floor," said Ry. "I don't even know her, and I come into her house . . ." The end of the sentence was his hand gesturing toward where the floor used to be.

Del shrugged. "It was an accident waiting to happen," he said. "It's actually lucky we were here. It was lucky it was you, not Miles.

"You should try to get some sleep on the couch," he said then. "That way, when I finish this, you can drive and I can sleep. Then we can make up for the lost time."

So Ry went out to the couch. He pulled a red fuzzy throw over himself and laid his head on a corduroy pillow. (Did you hear about the guy who fell asleep on the corduroy pillow? It made headlines.) He was becoming like a dog, he thought, that can curl up anywhere and fall asleep. After a few minutes, he found another pillow to put over his head to muffle the sawing and hammering. Because he wasn't quite like a dog. He didn't have a furry, floppy ear.

# CONCURRENTLY
# (THAT SAME NIGHT),
# ALSO IN THE MIDWEST
# (CON-PLACENTLY?)

Lloyd was being taken somewhere in the backseat of a car. The highway was a blur; the exits were all generically named and populated with Comfort Inns, BP gas plazas, and whatnot, all with signage glowing into the night. The car left the highway for a briefly busy thoroughfare lined with car dealerships, big box stores, and fast food franchises that soon dwindled to a county road. There had been some social events, with people he didn't know, but he didn't feel unsafe. He was with Betty and her sister.

The car slowed and turned onto a dirt two-track. The two-track jolted and meandered haphazardly into a thicket, which thinned and heightened and spread into a woods, which dimmed into a forest.

The bumpiness of the road did not soothe a dull throbbing Lloyd felt at the back of his head. The car crept along behind its headlights. He closed his eyes. When, after a time, the car rolled to a stop, he didn't notice. What woke him was the clunk and squeak of the car door opening next to him, and the cool air from outside. It was falling asleep that threw him off. His recovering brain cells had not had time to regroup. Disoriented by sleep and by his skipping synapses, he looked to see who had opened his door, but the inside of the car was lit and it was dark beyond; black as ink, black as pitch. As black as night, you could say. He heard footsteps walking away in pine needles and soft earth, then a key being inserted into a lock. A door was opening, creaking lightly. He wondered if he was in danger; a memory fragment surfaced, something about a car pulling up beside him as he walked on an unfamiliar sidewalk, the apprehensiveness he felt as he turned to see who it was. He wondered whether he shouldn't disappear silently into the darkness, the pitchy inky night. While he had the chance, he swung his feet out and down to the ground. He stood up and stepped out of the circle of light.

"Where did he go?" said Betty to her sister, Ruth.

They were twins, but they had different dispositions. Betty was cheery and friendly, Ruth was more on the cranky side.

They were searching through the dark woods with

flashlights, trying not to get lost themselves.

"I guess I shouldn't have brought him there," said Betty. "It was probably confusing with all those people. I just thought—"

"If you would mind your own business," said Ruth, "you'd save yourself a lot of trouble. Not to mention other people."

Oh, shut up, Ruth, thought Betty. "I hope he's not lying facedown in a ditch somewhere," she said.

Which, oddly enough, Lloyd was. Five minutes into his escape, his head cleared, and he remembered: Betty, the neighbor. The family cabin.

Feeling foolish, he turned to go back. He could see the tiny windows lighting up in the cabin in the distance. He felt for the ground with his feet and held his hands in front of him to fend off unseen branches. What tripped him up was a half-fallen sapling, at shin height. He came up against it and went down like a mousetrap snapping shut. He had just enough time to put out his arms and break his fall. Thus fracturing his collarbone. And one of his wrists.

So, technically, there wasn't a ditch, Ruth might have said.

To which we say, Oh, shut up, Ruth.

## AND NOW
## BACK TO RY,
## SLEEPING ON SHARON'S COUCH

His sleep was not quite as restful as it might have been had he slept next to a radio stuck between stations, or under the dripping pipe on the kitchen before Del fixed it. His dreams made their way over a soggy, wafer-thin floor littered with obstacles. Phones were ringing in faraway rooms. He needed to find them and answer them, but the noise he had to move through made it hard to figure out where they were. The phones would tell him what it was that he was supposed to do. Time and again he was on the verge of finding one when it turned out to be something else. Chirping birds in a cage. An alarm clock. A microwave oven announcing that the burrito was warmed up now. He took the burrito out of the microwave. The microwave was in a gas station convenience store. Someone grabbed his arm and said,

"Hey," and he realized that the burrito belonged to that person. It was Del. The burrito belonged to Del. Del was shaking his arm gently, and he opened his eyes and it really was Del.

"I think we better get going," said Del.

You have to be asleep for someone to wake you up, so Ry must have slept, but he felt woozy and unrested. He eased up to a sitting position and leaned his face into his hands, not ready for the lamplight Del had switched on. After an indeterminate amount of time, he pushed his way up into a standing position. The swath of pain that flashed through his groin as he did so went a long way toward waking him up more thoroughly. He walked stiffly toward the kitchen and squinted into its fluorescent brightness.

It was tidy as a pin. Whatever that means. The heap of rubbish had been removed, and in front of the sink was a sturdy, neatly built mosaic of pieces of wood Del had found in the basement. They were different colors. It looked kind of cool, really. Like if people saw it, they would want one, too. Ry went over and stood on it. Solid as a rock. Then he stepped back and pulled open the cabinet door. A similarly crafted level surface held up the bottles and buckets and whatever else was underneath there.

"We should go," Del said again. He looked tired, but happy. They turned out the light in the kitchen and the lamp in the living room and stepped out the front door and pulled it shut with a quiet click. The screen door banged lightly behind them. The world had freshened up overnight: the air was cool and moist, a couple of birds sang back and forth, a new sky had barely begun its glimmering over at the horizon.

Del climbed behind the wheel and Ry thought maybe he had decided to drive after all. But he only navigated the twists and turns to the on-ramp, then pulled over.

"I probably won't sleep more than a couple of hours," he said. "We're on this road for quite a ways now, so all you have to do is stay on it." He crawled over the seat into the back. Ry slid over into the driver's seat. He fastened his seatbelt and heard Del's boots come off and land on the floor, heard Del sliding down into his bag and arranging himself.

"Wake me up for breakfast," Del said. So Ry put the Willys in gear and headed up onto the highway.

# YOU ARE HERE

It was exhilarating to be alone at the helm. At first it was enough just to be driving down the highway. The time of day itself was kind of amazing. It wasn't often that Ry was doing anything useful at this hour. Not that many other people were either, apparently; traffic was sparse. He felt himself one of a small brotherhood: The Few. The Proud. The Awake.

The sun rose orange from the edge of a clear sky and the countryside went all golden and emerald around him, with houses and barns set here and there catching the light and casting deep westerly shadows.

And then it was regular morning. Still nice, but less spectacular. Feeling an urge to put something in his mouth, Ry took a sip of his beverage from the night before, a blend of root beer, Sprite, Hawaiian Punch, and

Coke. It tasted pretty lousy. It was better when it was fresh and had carbonation. Or maybe it was an evening/morning thing. He tried a sip of Del's leftover beverage, a coffee. Bleahh. Even worse. He would have to hold off for a while.

It wouldn't be bad to have the radio on, though. He could play it softly. His eyes dropped momentarily down to the dashboard. Like many other parts of the Willys, the radio had been recruited from some other career and installed in a way that was obvious and made perfect sense to Del. Anyone else had to look at it for a minute or two and experiment a little. Open the mind to new possibilities. Think of all the ways a thing might be switched on.

I'm not saying that Ry didn't keep glancing up to make sure he was on the road, staying in his lane. But he wasn't looking at signs. He didn't think he had to. They were staying on the same road. For quite a ways. But sometimes, staying on the same road means you have to choose the left part of a Y or take an exit to the left side of the road. Sometimes both, in quick succession. Sometimes you have to look at the signs to get where you want to go.

He found a decent station and settled back in. The

highway had widened—it had six lanes now—and it was getting busier. A lot of trucks barreled past and moved in and out of lanes behind him and ahead of him. The trucks were like planets with their own gravity; he could feel his own course being altered when they roared by. Too close for comfort. He heightened his powers of concentration. It was like Need for Speed. In Sensurround. He was glad he had turned on the radio. Tunes made him feel braver. More confident.

You can get used to anything. Before long Ry was unfazed by the vehicular tonnage careening all around him. He found the Flow. Serenely, his eyes took in his surroundings in a video game kind of way. In the present tense. Respond to what pops up in front of you.

It popped into his head that it was surprising that they weren't driving more into the sun, since they were heading southeast. The sun was actually behind them. They were heading west. But roads often twist and turn. Though this one seemed straight enough.

What felt good was, he was doing what needed to be done. He wasn't waiting for someone else to do it for him. It's true that he couldn't be doing it without Del, but he was doing his part, too. They were going to figure it all out. Find out the facts. They were on the way.

He drove under one of those overhead signs that tell which lane you should be in depending on where you are going. He looked at this one and couldn't help noticing that none of the choices applied to him, to them, to their plan. And then suddenly the road was splitting into three strands, each veering off in a radically different direction—right/left, up/down, over/under—lanes of traffic coming from every which way, and Ry had no idea where he should go.

He rode the traffic like a wave, deciding that survival was the main thing, but looking for clues, for the sign with his name on it. He was supposed to stay on the same road. Maybe this was just part of it. But the number wasn't right. The cities weren't right.

Calmness had left him, but he drove on. He couldn't exactly stop. Not in the middle of the spaghetti. His road dipped under and curved around and shot out high above a river, and then as quickly as he had entered the tangled knot he was out of it. Driving through the countryside. The wrong countryside, he was pretty sure.

Salvation came in the form of a highway rest area. He pulled off just so he could stop for a minute and think. Del's voice came from behind him, asking sleepily if it was time for breakfast.

"No," said Ry. "Not yet. I just have to . . ."

He got out of the Willys, leaving Del to fill in the blank. Walking inside the building, he glanced to his right and saw the giant map. The Blessed Map. The difference between this map and Del's road atlas was that this one had the magical You Are Here arrow. Fortunately, the map was large enough to include not only Where He Was, but Where He Was Supposed To Be. That was not shown by an arrow, but he found it. He didn't know how he had strayed. He was just glad he could find a hypotenusal route to get him back there that avoided the splitting, weaving rat's nest of roads he had just clenched his way through.

He zipped to the restroom, then returned to the map and studied it again. He memorized what he had to do. There were three parts to it. Three road numbers, plus three town names where he made changes. He made up a singsongy rhyme to help him remember. It had the three parts, then it went, uh-huh, oh yeah, or la la la or something. Some beats to finish it off.

When he started up the Jeep, Del's voice asked, "Are we there yet?"

Ry said, "No, go back to sleep." Realizing he had been abrupt, he added, "I mean, I think we should go a little farther."

He made his way back into the stream of traffic. The

first change came up almost right away. He guided the Willys into the lane under the desired route number and curved smoothly to the south while the other lane continued stubbornly, misguidedly west. The rhyme song shrank to two main parts. More filler. La la la la la, shaboom, shaboom.

He didn't want Del to know he had messed up. He didn't want Del to save him this time. He wanted to fix it himself. He didn't have any clear idea of how long he had been going the wrong way or how long it would be till they were right again. It was twelve miles to the next change, according to the sign. A few eons passed, then it was five miles. One mile. And now, here was the exit. Here was the road that would lead them to the right road. This road was a secondary road. It rambled along from one tiny town to another. It had potholes. It had traffic lights.

Ry aimed for maximum smoothness. He tried to smoothly swerve around the potholes. Some of them were canyons that trenched across both lanes. Sometimes the abundance of them didn't allow for weaving. You just had to jolt through as damage-free as possible. He eased to a halt as smoothly as he could when the lights went red and, as smoothly as he could, shifted back up to speed when they went green.

He watched for signs telling him how far he still needed to go. He knew he was running out of time, if he wanted his goof-up to remain undiscovered. More potholes, a spattering of them. Bada boom. Shaboom, shaboom, la la la boom. It was an anti-lullaby. An un-lullaby, like machine-gun fire.

And another intersection: Stop. Wait. Start.

A newly paved stretch of asphalt appeared and slipped itself beneath the wheels. The sudden quiet was velvety; it was like church. A sign rose up and announced that only one mile remained until the elusive, conclusive junction. And then there it was. The on-ramp curling gracefully ahead and to the right. Ry put on the turn signal. Victory flowed through his veins. He had done it. He had found his way back. Choirs of angels gathered on pinheads and sang. Del would never know. La la la la la la la.

"It looks like we're almost out of gas," Del said. Ry flew up out of his skin, bumped his head on the ceiling, and almost went off the road. That is, two of those things seemed to happen and one of them did happen.

"We'd better get some before we get back on the highway," said Del. He was leaning over the back of the passenger seat. How long had he been there? Ry stayed on the road but missed the ramp. He made the sound of raspberries at the exit, the road ahead, his doomed effort.

"Well, we won't get very far without it," Del said. "Look, there's a place right there. And we can get breakfast.

"Where are we, anyway?" he asked. "Why are we off the highway?"

And Ry realized that maybe Del still didn't know what had happened. He made a couple more raspberries, the sound of a motor puttering along.

"Detour," he said. "I think there was an accident."

He was just summarizing. It was one way of putting it.

# DOGS

I DON'T THINK THIS IS RIGHT. I NEVER SAW ANYTHING
LIKE THIS.  AND IT DOESN'T SMELL FAMILIAR AT ALL.

WE WERE PROBABLY SLEEPING IN THIS PART.  I BET
WE'RE ALMOST THERE.

THIS IS TAKING A LONG TIME.

THAT'S BECAUSE WE'RE WALKING.  WE CAME THE OTHER WAY IN
THE CAR, REMEMBER?

I GUESS SO.

THIS DOESN'T LOOK
RIGHT, EITHER.

## TENNESSEE.
## GEORGIA.
## FLORIDA.

There was highway ahead and highway behind.

Somewhere in the afternoon, while Del was behind the wheel, Ry noticed how the sun made funky shadows of the stairs curving up around a grove of giant cylindrical storage tanks.

He said to Del, "So, is Yulia, like, your girlfriend or something?"

So much time passed before Del answered that Ry thought maybe he hadn't heard the question, and then he wondered if he had even said it aloud or only thought it.

Then Del said, "I guess you would say she's my ex-girlfriend. She's still a girl, and she's still willing to be my friend, but not my *girlfriend*."

"Do you still like her, though?" Ry asked. Because he got the feeling Del did.

"Once I'm smitten, I seem to stay smitten," said Del. "At least until something else smites me. Or someone."

Ry wanted to ask, So why did she dump you? But he thought that might be too personal. Del told him anyway.

"I guess I drove her nuts," he said.

"Like how?" asked Ry. "What did you do?"

Del shrugged. "She thought I was too stubborn," he said. "But I don't see it that way."

Ry didn't see it that way either.

"I don't think you're stubborn," he said. "At least, not in a bad way. Except maybe about pickles."

Del's face did its invisible smiling thing.

"That's only because you haven't known me very long," he said. "I've been compared to a brick wall. Among other things."

"So, you are stubborn?" asked Ry.

"I never said I wasn't stubborn," said Del. "I only said I wasn't *too* stubborn."

A number of pine trees whipped by. A mind-boggling number. Maybe an infinite number. An imaginary, abstract number. The dirt was red and the land was flat. There were billboards about pecans. This went on for quite a while: hours. Eons.

"So, is the airplane really homemade?" asked Ry.

Del smiled. "There are different levels of homemade," he said. "It's not like we'll be riding bicycles and flapping our arms. Would you feel better if I said it was hand built by a brilliant and meticulous aerospace engineer?"

"Uh-huh," said Ry. "I would."

"Well, it's not exactly like that, either," said Del. "It's somewhere in between."

A few minutes later, he said, "Closer to the engineer than to the bicycle."

And after another minute he said, "But maybe not by much."

Palm trees and twinkling lights erupted from the gathering darkness. The stars that are always out there, even in the daytime, could now be seen in the dimming airy pool of the sky. Traffic ripped along around them, pushing and pulling. A full day of riding with the windows open had long ago blown away any crispiness; the morning had happened years ago. Still, they had to keep going. They weren't there yet.

As much as Ry was tired of sitting in a car, he wasn't sure he even wanted to get there. He wasn't exactly sure about this next part, with the airplane.

The night air was humid, but not unpleasant. It was

soft, but insistent, caressing his face like the tongues of an infinite number of puppies. Ry closed his eyes and became one with the air, and the seat he was molded to, and the radio station that was playing. It was an oldies radio station, which he was not usually so fond of, but he became one with it anyway. He let it empty out his mind of everything but danceable field reports from the battleground of love. Plus some outliers on other topics— the science fiction future, cheeseburgers, haircuts. Del sampled his way up and down the dial, then switched it off. Ry became one with the absence of the radio. He became one with dozing off.

He was awakened by a change in velocity, then a stop. Ry squinted out the window, not willing to open his eyes the whole way. They were moving again, but they had left the highway. The missing roar of rushing air and traffic felt at first like silence, but it wasn't. The relative stillness of the air meant you could smell things, non-automotive things: Growth. Efflorescence. Perfume of flowers. The sea. Musk of animals. Stench of decaying same. Alligators. Burgers.

At three A.M. they turned and crunched quietly into a gravel driveway. Del turned off the engine. Black nutrient-rich night poured silently into the car. The air was heavy enough to pin a person down, but both Ry and Del had by now accumulated irrepressible desires to stand up, and they opened their doors and stood. That was all, for a minute or two. Standing, looking up, around, stretching the arms up overhead.

It may have been the siren call of exposed-armpit aroma that beckoned to the mosquitos. More likely they were just a standard ingredient of the air here. They seemed to account for roughly 10 percent of it. Definitely enough to qualify as a pollutant in the form of suspended particulate. Or even a plague. Probably not a plague.

One window glowed faintly. Ry walked closer to peer inside, through the horizontal slats of old-fashioned venetian blinds. The window was open. Moths fluttered from the screen as Ry came near, then made their returns to it. The back side of someone's head, lit by a shaded lamp, was half obscured by the back of an easy chair, like the sun half hidden at the horizon. An electric fan hummed on a nearby tabletop. It fluffed the hair on the head, then let it fall as it oscillated to and fro, left and right, side to side. Fluff, fall, fluff, fall. A hand reached for a glass on the table, then replaced it and disappeared. Ry tiptoed back.

"Someone's awake," he said, smearing yet another

soft-bodied insect blood-wise across his face. A sharp, quiet slap sounded from the direction of Del, who said, "I hope Everett's house has an air lock."

As they headed for what they could make out as the door of the house, it was suddenly illuminated by a porch light. A buzzer went off somewhere inside. The door behind the screen door was open, and the click of dog toenails on a linoleum floor came toward them. Followed by the silhouette of a man, back lit by motion-activated recessed lights in the ceiling of a hallway. The lights didn't come on until he had already passed under them, so they didn't see his face until he reached the screen door. Even then, the porch light mainly lit up the screen itself. He remained mostly in silhouette. He was shortish. And he was wearing shorts. That's all Ry could tell.

Along with activating the porch light, the sound of the car doors and/or their approach had activated a couple of bug zappers at the corners of the porch. They zapped sharply, in quick succession. Ry jumped as if he had stepped on a live wire, turning as he did to see and hear the glowing violet zappers take down two more victims.

When he landed and thought to turn back, Everett had opened the door and was inviting them in. He and Del exchanged "hellos" as if it were only mildly surprising to appear on someone's doorstep from out of nowhere, in the wee hours of the morning. Ry trailed behind them down the hallway, which had gone dark again but now relit as they passed. He saw that the lights were aimed at pictures that hung on the walls on one side. But if he stood still to look at them, the lights went out. He had to kind of shift back and forth to keep the light on.

There were four pictures, four lights in the ceiling. The first light shone on a painting of a shipwreck. It was a real painting, and it looked old. Maybe because the frame looked old; it was golden and ornate, and pieces of it had broken off. But the painting looked old, too. The colors had a nostalgic yellowed cast, and a lot of it was just dark, one part indistinguishable from the next. But some of the water around the boat was catching the light. The waves heaved up in a translucent emerald that suggested the darkness below was cold and deep and wet and forbidding. A few people huddled on the end of the boat that still protruded from the water, waiting their turn to ride the breeches buoy, the bucket with leg holes sliding along a thick rope knotted onto a mast. Would they get their turn? Hard to say. Within the painting, they were doomed to huddle and wait forever.

Ry shuffled sideways to the next one. This was an

engraving, also old, of a train derailment. Hey, Everett, cheery theme. To be specific, the engraving showed the front part of the train dangling from a bridge. A trestle. Passengers were disembarking from the part of the train that was still earth based, still on the track, like ants when the anthill is flooded. In the foreground a few of them had opened a picnic basket and spread a cloth on the ground. One of them, a woman in a voluminous dress covered in tiny stripes going every which way as the fabric folded on itself, gazed pensively at the dangling engine as she sipped a glass of wine. In her other hand, she held a drumstick of the poultry variety. She was coping.

Light off, light on. The third picture was a black-and-white photograph of an erupting volcano. Ry thought it was erupting. Maybe it was just smoking. Immense puffy gray clouds hovered in the air, obscuring the mouth, the crater. A village lay scattered over the slopes at the base of the mountain. Lights were on in the village; the clouds of ash had darkened the sky. Ry drew closer to see if people were fleeing, but the motion-sensor spotlight didn't like that and cut him off. He stepped back. Couldn't tell, too far away. He danced sideways to the last picture. What would it be? The Fire of London? The San Francisco Earthquake?

But here it seemed Everett had abandoned his theme. This one was a photo, too, but it was just a candid snapshot of a woman looking over her shoulder at the camera, laughing. Almost like a motion-sensor soundtrack, the sound of laughter came to Ry's ears. But it was male laughing. Everett and Del. Where were they? He peeked around a doorway into the room he had observed through the venetian blinds, but it was empty.

On the far side of the room, another doorway opened onto what turned out to be a screened porch. Ry could see Del's foot at the end of what he deduced would turn out to be Del's leg. He headed on over. The room he passed through was a living room. The fan oscillated, with a light variable drone, sending vague wafts of warm air around its ninety-degree purview. The breezes that distributed the dust and dog hair on the floor were a science fair–sized version of the forces that shape sand dunes. But the room was dim and Ry walked, in shoes, over a portion of the surface swept bare by the winds. He didn't notice the drifts forming elsewhere.

He did notice a sharp pungency reeking in from the left and was surprised to see, when he turned, that it came from a kitchen. A teakettle boiled merrily on the stove top. Ry stepped in and turned it off. A mug with a tea bag waited on the counter. So he filled it with boiling water and carried it along with him.

On the porch, in the dark, Everett and Del were discussing Everett's methane digester. Everett had a couple of pigs, Rob and Inga, and he was using their manure as a source of gas for his stove and his water heater. But he had taken a shortcut in the venting part of the process. Hence the aroma. It didn't really bother him. He wasn't in a hurry to fix it. It did what he needed it to do.

Everett's voice was jolly. He laughed wholeheartedly at his own jokes, at Del's jokes; he laughed when Ry brought him the mug of tea. Each time Everett laughed, or anyone, though it was Everett who laughed the most, a sound-activated light flickered on overhead and stayed on for about ten seconds. Probably it wasn't designed to be about laughing; probably it was for coming out with your hands full, maybe carrying a tray of food, and you could make a noise, the light would turn on, and you could see where you were going. But for now it was triggered by Everett laughing. It was like watching a series of blackout sketches called "The Everett and Del Show."

The first few times the lights flashed on, Ry looked

at Everett, because he hadn't seen him clearly yet. He looked bearded and sunburned, kind of shaggy. One hand absentmindedly scratched the head of his dog, who lay next to him, its head on Everett's thigh. *Her* head. Her name was Lulu. She was a mutt with a collie-esque profile.

Ry gathered that Everett and Del had known each other for a long time. They had climbed mountains together. They had jumped out of airplanes and down into caves. Rafted churning rivers.

That was all a long time ago. But those are the kind of things that, once you do them with someone, you can show up on their doorstep anytime during the rest of your life and ask for an airplane ride.

"You'll have to help me put a new wing on," said Everett. "Actually, I'm glad you're both here to help with that. I'd have a hard time doing it by myself."

"What happened to the wing?" asked Del.

"Oh, I had a small mishap," said Everett. "I was coming back from Yulia's, and I ran into some weather. The engine started acting up, and I had to make an alternate landing in a field. It was getting dark, and I was concentrating on avoiding some utility wires. I didn't even notice this old water tank in the middle of the field. Took the wing right off."

219

He laughed, and the lights flickered on.

Ry had not said much. He had been listening, half listening, really, waiting to receive his couch assignment. Maybe he would just sleep in this chair, sitting up. Now. Or wander back into the living room and assess the couch situation there.

This story caught his attention, though. His chin lifted right off his chest. It was the kind of story where your first reaction was, Holy crap. Were you okay? And then your second reaction might be, And this is the plane we're going to be flying in? And you're driving?

But Del just said, "From Yulia's?" It seemed to Ry that Del's voice, and his features, were carefully neutral. Probably he didn't want Ry to panic about the plane, thinking about all the things that could go wrong. Probably he was trying to change the subject.

# AIRPLANE DAY

Everything seems more normal in the morning. This time only for about a minute, though. Ry opened his eyes and registered his surroundings. He was on another couch. That was okay. It was a glider, actually; an old-fashioned piece of furniture that moved backward and forward a little. The glider was on a screened-in porch. The air wafted balmy over his skin. It was nice.

Ry thought he could hear the sound of the surf and sat up to find out whether he could see the ocean. The sound turned out to be coming from a blowtorch. Everett, in a Hawaiian shirt, his skinny legs, and flip-flops, was weeding his patio. With some kind of blowtorch-flamethrower device. It seemed to be effective: ahead of him weeds surged from between the patio stones in cocky throngs. Behind him they shriveled, scorched and defeated. At least for now. The stones were scorched, too.

As Ry watched in fascination, Everett switched the blowtorch to his left hand, so that he could reach into the pocket of his shorts with his right and pull out a cell phone. As he held it to his ear, his attention drifted to what he was hearing, his glance turned upward, and the aim of the flame strayed within igniting distance of a crumpled paper plate that Ry hadn't noticed until it burst into flame. The burning wad scooted away, propelled by the flame jet, toward a loose coil of twine. Which also ignited.

Ry's gaze sought out the other end of the twine. He was sitting up straight now. The twine burned along like a fuse. In a way, it *was* a fuse. Everett hadn't seen the plate or the twine ignite. He was listening intently, his eyes once again looking down toward his patio weeding task. The twine fuse burned along behind and away from him. Ry pulled his shoes on. He would go trample it out.

About fifteen feet from the house, a large metal oil drum stood in scrubby grass, with a smaller oil drum nestled upside down inside the top of it. A plastic hose looped its way from the top drum over into the side of the house. A few coils of the twine had wedged between the plastic hose and the patio. The ball of twine itself sat just beyond that, in a rat's nest of tools and scraps, next to some rusted contraptions that resembled extinct mechanical livestock, grazing on an un-mowed island of meadow.

Ry hurried out the door. He wanted to trample the burning twine before it got to the rat's nest. It had already reached the coils under the plastic hose.

Suddenly Everett whooshed past in a few leaping strides. He yanked the plastic hose out from the house and tossed it to the ground, then leaped toward Ry in a few more uber-strides. He grabbed Ry's shoulders to push him away. The burning twine melted a hole in the plastic hose. Almost instantly there was a mighty *WHOMP!* and the smaller oil drum flew high into the air with a brilliant flash of fire. It hovered up there for a second or so before it came clanging back down. Meanwhile, the twine fuse burned over to the scrap heap. It ignited some scraps of cardboard, then a heap of wood chips and before long, a lively bonfire was under way.

"Damn!" said Everett. He bolted around the corner of the house and returned with a garden hose to soak down the scrap heap. The hose he had yanked from the house lay smoldering and smoking on the patio, partially melted, and cooling into a new shape.

"What happened?" asked Del, appearing barefoot in the doorway. The patio stones and the weeds Everett had scorched on purpose made the scene look even more dramatic.

"My methane digester exploded," said Everett. Aside from that one "Damn," he didn't seem too perturbed. Then he said, "Jeez, I bet that scared Lulu. She hates explosions." Now he did seem worried, and he headed around the house, looking around and calling for the dog.

# THE
# LONGEST
# BREAKFAST

Everett returned shortly, carrying the quivering Lulu in his arms. He set her down on a nest of blankets and wiped his hands on his shorts. Because the stove was out of commission, thanks to the explosion, he dug out an electric skillet.

"Eggs?" he asked. "Pancakes? Both?"

He proceeded to mix up a batch of pancake batter, throwing in a little of this, a lot of that. He scooped and dumped with a carefree flair, as if he had done this many times and knew exactly how to do it. Or else he was completely oblivious to the idea that amounts might matter. It was hard to tell which.

He asked Del to start cooking the pancakes while he, Everett, got Ry started on the squeezing of the orange juice. The orange juice squeezer was old-fashioned, with a handle that went up and down. Everett dragged a crate of oranges over from the corner and found a sharp knife for Ry to cut them in half with.

"This batter looks like cement," observed Del.

"You might want to turn the heat down on the skillet," Everett observed back at him. Mainly because he had observed the column of smoke rising from the hot oil. Maybe he felt one fire-related incident per morning, per house, was enough.

"I always do it this way," said Del. "They come out just right."

He poured four sizzling circles of batter, *PSSsssh, PSsssshw, PSSSshw, Psshw*. Everett glanced over from where he was scooping coffee into a paper filter.

"The insides won't get cooked," he said. "And the outsides will burn."

Del ignored this. Instead, he said to Ry, "See if you can find a sieve to pour that through and get the pulp out."

"The pulp is the best part," said Everett. "It's the fiber.

"I do have a sieve, though," he said. "I even know where it is. I used it yesterday, to get the ants out of the syrup."

He fished it out of the sink, tapped it to knock out the remaining ant carcasses, gave it a rinse, and set it on the counter near Ry. Del flipped the pancakes. The cooked sides were dark. Very, very dark. Ry kept chopping and squeezing. And now, straining.

Lulu had recovered. She wandered over and sat next to the crate of oranges, watching Ry. He reached down for another orange and gave her a scratch, forgetting that his hand was sticky with juice and pulp. When he brought his hand away, it was covered with dog hair.

"Interesting," said Everett, cutting into the crispy pancakes with the side of his fork. Moist batter oozed out, glistening. He scraped up the gooey part with the crispy part and put it in his mouth.

He didn't say, "Mmm." No one did.

"I don't know what happened," said Del. "Maybe the coils in your skillet aren't heating evenly."

"Could be," said Everett. Graciously, Ry thought.

"The batter was pretty thick, too," said Del. "Do you ever measure anything?"

"Measuring is for sissies," said Everett. Not quite as graciously.

"Or the thermostat might be off," said Del. "It can be off just a little and it will make a big difference." Okay, Del, you can shut up now, thought Ry.

"You don't go by the thermostat," said Everett. "You go by what's happening with the oil in the pan." With an unspoken *any idiot knows that*.

Jeez, Ry thought. It's just pancakes.

He took a crispy, gooey bite, slathered in butter and syrup. It wasn't exactly pancakes.

"Mmm," he said. "Calories. I love calories."

Ry decided a new topic would be good.

"Hey," he said. "What was the coolest thing you guys ever did together?" He felt like a kindergarten teacher. Play nice, everyone.

At first it seemed his ploy had worked. Del and Everett agreed immediately on a particular climbing trip, in the Rockies. They waxed poetic: starting the climb in the dark, the first glow in the east. The huge quiet of the mountains, with only the scraping of the crampons and the slight sound of the ropes whispering into knots. Looking out from the top to see one peak after another.

Before long, they were remembering a particular cave in the side of a mountain, where they had taken shelter one cold and stormy night. They decided to try to build something of a wall, to keep the howling winds out, using the ready supply of rocks all around them.

Sitting inside their sleeping bags for warmth, they would reach around for a rock, then lean forward to place it carefully on their wall. They could not agree now on which one of them had chosen the rock that was too large, too irregular, and too sharp, and who had set that rock on top of the wall. They couldn't agree on who had said, "That's going to fall and rip holes in our bags." Which it then did. Not big holes. Just big enough to argue about.

Ry watched them bat it back and forth across the table for about twenty minutes. What is it with these guys, he thought. Who even cares who picked the bad rock? It was a mistake. He couldn't quite believe how . . . *stubborn* Del was being. Everett was being stubborn, too.

Ry broke in. "I'm sorry to interrupt," he said, "but do you think I could use your phone, Everett?"

"Oh, sure," said Everett amiably. He pulled it out of his pocket and handed it to Ry.

"I'll go outside," said Ry. As he left the kitchen, Everett and Del resumed their argument.

No one answered at the house. No surprise, though he had hoped. He pushed the buttons to retrieve messages. There was only one, from the police: Had he heard anything? He called the number and left his own message: "No."

Del and Everett walked past, talking and laughing, on their way to the big pole barn where Everett kept the airplane.

Okay, he thought. So maybe they won't kill each other.

# HERE WE GO, THEN

Except for being so small and for missing one wing, it looked like a regular airplane. Until you got close, and then especially when you looked inside and saw the duct tape everywhere. Then it looked like a refrigerator-box spaceship made by a six-year-old. Only less roomy. The dashboard instruments appeared to be authentic. But, Ry thought, how would I know?

"I know duct tape is really great," he said, "but I didn't know it could hold airplanes together."

"The duct tape isn't holding anything together," Everett reassured him. "It just reduces some of the vibration. Sort of. Well, I don't know if it actually does that, but that's what I wanted it to do. It gets pretty loud up there. Sometimes I can't hear for days."

A person might think it would take quite a while to

attach a wing to an airplane, roll it out the door, and take off. That is, if you could even do it at all. Some part of a person might be secretly hoping you couldn't. But it seemed to happen zipzapzoop, just like that. Before Ry knew it.

Even in that short time, Del and Everett found a lot to disagree about. For example, every little thing.

"Four-inch bolt?" Del would ask.

"No, I think a three-inch will do it," Everett would answer. You could reverse who said what; it happened both ways.

"You sure?" asked Del.

"Yup," answered Everett.

"It's your life," said Del.

"It's our life, too," said Ry. Everett chuckled. Ry felt more nervous.

He was starting to get that the arguing might not mean that much. It made him nervous anyway.

Or maybe that had more to do with this little airplane.

Ry couldn't decide whether it was good that the three of them could lift the wing up into position, because that meant it was lightweight and would be more likely to stay up in the air, or if it was bad, because that meant it was flimsy, not trustworthy.

He had flown before, in big commercial aircraft,

without giving it much thought. But the metal of Everett's airplane was not all curved and aerodynamic. The bends were angular, as if they had been folded along some giant dotted line. Who knows, maybe they were. Maybe that was how it was actually done.

He asked Everett. Who laughed.

"Yes," said Everett. "It's an origami airplane."

He moved around the plane, checking, tugging, tightening, in such a matter-of-fact way. It was calming. But then, there they were, strapped into the tiny silvery cubbyhole cockpit, barreling down the runway, which was just a field, really, with some orange cones and a wind sock on the far side of the pole barn. Ry wished they could just drive the whole way.

They had liftoff. The earth fell away.

"Here we go, then," said Everett.

"Up, up, and away," said Del.

Once they were aloft and vibrating, Everett mentioned that the forecast in the newspaper yesterday had been for good flying weather.

"We're flying an airplane on a forecast from yesterday's newspaper?" asked Del.

"They usually come pretty close," said Everett. "Not always, of course."

They motored through the air, inching along above the glittering seas in their dinky aluminum husk. Ry could see their insignificant shadow on the water way down below. The noise seemed more solid than the plane itself.

Lulu was along for the ride, squished in next to Ry. She wore specially designed dog ear protectors, on stretchy fabric that went around her head. She might be freaked out by explosions, but she seemed unfazed by flying in small airplanes. She seemed calm. But she was a dog. What did she know?

Everett shouted, over the noise of the engine, that the last time he flew over to Yulia's, the air had been really bumpy.

"And the time before that," he said, "I was running just ahead of a thunderstorm. So today is just great. Picture-perfect."

"Do you go there pretty often?" asked Del. He shouted it in an offhanded way. But Yulia was his old girlfriend. Who he still liked. Was smitten with. Ry leaned forward slightly to hear what Everett might say.

"Well, I go there once a week or so for work," he said. "I have a sort of a job there. And I usually stop in at Yulia's to say hello."

That seemed like an okay answer to Ry. His attention shifted to his stomach, where uncooked pancake batter was swiftly expanding, or creating $CO_2$ molecules or whatever baking powder and raw eggs do when they ripen together.

It occurred to Ry that there did not seem to be enough air in there for them all to be breathing. He knew this was all in his head, because he could breathe more easily by burying his face in Lulu's fur, which made no sense at all. Unless dog fur had hidden air pockets, like the ones seals have, to help them float. He kept his face in there for a while.

He lifted his head when Everett started banging on the dashboard, or whatever it was called.

"I thought I fixed that," Everett said in mild surprise.

"What is it?" asked Del.

"The dial isn't moving," said Everett, pointing. "I think it's just a loose connection. Can you pry that panel off and take a look? There's a screwdriver in that box under your seat."

This did not sound so good to Ry. He didn't think it would sound so good to Del, the meticulous craftsman,* either. He could almost hear Del spitting out the word *shoddy*.

*Except concerning pancakes. But even there, you can bet that Del's next batch would be better than the first.

But if there was anything Del liked better than fixing things, it was fixing things while in a precarious situation. Rising to the occasion. Being more than a passive passenger. He was happy as a clam.

Ry, on the other hand, noticed that red itchy bumps were appearing on his skin. Hives. All over. He sat, cramped, sweaty, waiting, and now, itching.

Glancing out the window reminded him that things could be worse.

At least the plane is still in the air, he thought to himself. At least I'm not sick to my stomach. Though when he thought that, he realized he easily could be, so he tried to think a different thought as soon as he could.

At least . . . at least I don't have any broken bones.

At least Lulu is here.

At least I'm not hungry. Though hungry might be better.

At least—at least I'm not—like, a political prisoner.

Okay, he didn't want to play that game anymore. He was hot. He was itchy. He fixed his gaze on a toggle switch that vibrated a few feet directly ahead of him. The plane was still noisy, but the steadiness of the loud droning was lulling. After a while, his mind wandered, and his gaze followed. For an hour or more, he forgot where he was, at least in a concrete way, even though he was watching islands of various sizes mosey by, far below, out the window. They were abstract islands.

Then the plane dipped down. The bottom fell out from under them. They fell into a layer of bumpy air that bounced them around like a shoe in a clothes dryer. Oh, good, Ry thought. Even better. He looked at Lulu, strapped in beside him. She tried to lick his face, as well as she could between ricochets, with the healing spit of dogs. Her breath was not that great. But she was his favorite part of what was happening.

It was hard to ignore that what was happening could include, at any second, something pretty bad.

"Rough patch of air," Del said to Everett.

"Like driving down a rocky road," said Everett. "Makes you realize that air is a real thing."

They didn't seem worried. Maybe Ry shouldn't worry, either. Okay.

But it was so unpredictable. And invisible. You couldn't see it coming. Smooth enough, and then WHAM. Or

DROP.

Worry didn't seem out of line. Still, he tried to ratchet it down. Direct it into problem-solving. What could he actually do? The first thing that popped into his mind was the unhelpful reminder that a person who is lost should stay in one place and wait to be found. Great. Another rule he had broken. Though he didn't think that would have—

Whoa . . . hang on . . . roller coaster . . .

Maybe it was time for large thoughts. He sent his love out into the rough air, hoping it would find its way to his family, his friends, his dogs. Wherever they all were. Put his arm around Lulu, surrogate for all of them. If he went down, he would go down with her.

Ry closed his eyes and thought about heaven. He believed that it was a still place, very still. It was on the ground, not in the clouds, and the angels didn't fly; they walked. There was grass, and there were trees. There were picnic tables and a concession stand and a souvenir shop. There were gravel paths and informational signs. Maybe he wasn't thinking of heaven. Maybe it was more like a state park.

He was headed for the concession stand when, through his reverie, he heard Everett say, "Here we go, then."

"We're landing on *that*?" asked Del's voice. "There's

a whole huge island down there and we're going to
land on a sidewalk balanced on a precipice? That's like
landing on the edge of a knife."

"Yeah," said Everett.

"Wow," said Del. "I hope we don't miss." He sounded
impressed. Ry considered opening his eyes. But didn't.

"I haven't missed yet," said Everett. "Though I guess
there's a first time for everything."

"Wouldn't it be easier to use a seaplane and just land
in the water?" asked Del. "Seems like it would leave you
more margin for error."

"Well, number one, that's not so easy in the ocean
as it is in a lake," said Everett. "Number two, at least on
land you can see where the rocks are. And number three,
I don't have one of those. Also, you can't just leave it
there and wander off."

A sharp, sudden blow jolted them from below as
the rubber met the runway. Then came the bouncing
ride and g-force of the little plane leaning back as it
struggled to come to a halt before screaming off the
other end.

Ry's eyes had involuntarily opened. He saw some
land rolling off to one side, with vegetation and trees
growing out of it. Mountains, maybe, in the haze. He

could see the ocean, and they weren't in it. Everything was still, more or less.

"Cheated death again!" said Everett gaily. He opened the door and jumped down. Del followed. Everett poked his head back in and asked Ry to unstrap Lulu. Ry did so, and Lulu made her way to the door, where Everett helped her to the ground.

Then Ry crawled out and jumped down. His knees were wobbly. They didn't want to hold him up. He leaned over to unbend some of the kinks and creases that had formed. He had an urge to kiss the ground. In gratitude, sort of, for having made it. Then it seemed silly. And then it didn't. He didn't want Everett and Del to see him do it, though. He kept stretching, watching from the corner of his eye until they started walking away together toward one of the two buildings sitting off to the side of the runway. Then, quick as a wink, he put his lips to the sun-warmed asphalt or concrete or whatever it was. It was weird, but he felt better. He kissed the ground and thanked the sky. And jumped to his feet and followed the leaders. He lifted his T-shirt and looked at his stomach as he walked. Yowza. Bumps. Lulu had waited for him midway, and now she wagged her tail as he came near.

This airstrip, with the two small hangars to the side

of it, was part of a ritzy, private-type resort that people would fly into, in their ritzy, private-type airplanes. The airstrip and the unspoiled natural beauty were the only parts that existed so far. Everett was working for the guy who was "developing" the resort.

The developer lived in New York or New Jersey or somewhere.

Everett was mostly a landscaper, but he also worked with local subcontractors and laborers for the New York guy, because that guy didn't speak Spanish and Everett did.

He made a call now. Ry had taken Spanish in school, and he tried to follow what Everett said, but Everett was really good and it was like trying to pick words out of rifle fire.

Ry turned and looked back at the airstrip. They stood near one extremity of the island proper, but the first half of the runway, where they had touched down, was perched on a rocky promontory. The land fell sharply to the sea on either side of it. Ry was glad to be looking at this dramatic path of approach from down here, not from the air. He sent another kiss down to the earth through the soles of his feet. Hello. Thank you. I love you.

Everett had a Land Rover in the hangar. After they parked the airplane inside, they hopped in the Land Rover and headed for Yulia's. The road at one point ran close by the water and Ry said, "Hey, can I jump in the ocean, just for a minute?" He thought it might calm the itching.

And it did. While he was in the water, it was like heaven. Or a state park. But back in the Land Rover, as the salty water dried from his skin, he realized that now it was not only the rashy bumps that itched, but the clear skin between the rashy bumps and the parts of him that had no rash. He was a million (okay, eighteen) square feet of itch. He hoped that Yulia might have a bathtub and that he could excuse himself and remain submerged in unsalted water for the duration of the visit.

It was not a long ride. Soon they were in an old part of the city, where Yulia lived. Ry thought it looked European, though he had never been to Europe. European in island form. He would have liked to get out and walk around. For now, he just watched it all go by.

# AT YULIA'S

At the very moment that Ry met Yulia, he knew that he would be smitten by her, too. If he were older. He was half smitten now.

He could have fallen in love with just her voice; somehow it was like water when you were thirsty. When you had been hiking through heat and, out of nowhere, there appeared a waterfall. Or a merry brook with gravel on the bottom. Or a river. With rapids.

Her eyes were two different colors, but both of them glanced directly into his soul and laughed. With him, not at him. She moved in the graceful but unpredictable way that a deer moves. She was very warm, but there was a cool calmness to her, too. Within thirty minutes, the warmth and coolness of her presence had soothed away Ry's hives.

Bluff, fearless Everett, hale and hearty and reckless, sat quietly in a chair, his hands poised on his skinny legs as if he might push off any second. He spoke when Yulia asked him a question. Otherwise, he seemed almost shy. And pale. Ry happened to glance at him when Everett was glancing at Yulia while she was talking to Del. And what Ry thought when he saw that glance was, Everett is smitten.

I could be wrong, he thought. Maybe he's just having a minor stroke.

Del, in his Del way, was being useful. He offered to make some coffee, and he found some cookies and a pretty plate to put them on, and cups for everyone. While Yulia was explaining to Ry how *café tinto* was a little bit of coffee and a lot of milk, her cat waddled noisily into the kitchen. He was complaining, and he was wearing something and dragging it along the floor. It was his cat door. He wore it like a tutu. He was a fat cat and had gotten himself stuck in the opening on his way in to see who was visiting. So he yanked it from its moorings and brought it along.

Yulia laughed until tears rolled down her cheeks. Del lifted the unwieldy beast onto his lap and gently eased him from his new outfit. He apologized to the cat for Yulia's bad manners as he set him on the floor. Examining the cat door, which looked homemade, he said, "I think I could make this opening a little bigger."

He got up and went to a drawer in the counter and pulled it open. Riffling around, he found a small saber saw and sat back down to make the adjustment. He seemed at home in Yulia's kitchen. Lulu seemed at home in Yulia's kitchen, cat and all. Ry felt at home in Yulia's kitchen, too. Only Everett seemed ill at ease. Ry might not have noticed, except that this was so different now from before.

As they told Yulia of Ry's dilemma and their odyssey so far, and as Del asked to borrow her boat so they could go the final mile(s), the animals sensed that Everett was available. Lulu sat loyally on the floor beside him, nudging his hand with her head if he stopped caressing. The fat cat, Fred, leaped silently onto his lap to be stroked with the other hand. It seemed to work out well for all of them. Everett loosened up. His color returned. Maybe he had just had indigestion. The pancake batter. Ry could relate.

Before long, Everett looked down at his watch and said he guessed he'd better go.

"Okay," said Yulia.

"See you later, Everett," said Del. Only his legs and feet were visible in the kitchen. He was lying down on the floor, fitting the cat door back in its place. "Thanks for the lift."

"Are you going to fly back home today?" Ry asked, surprised. One ride a day in that thing seemed like plenty.

"Yep," said Everett. "And I have a few things to do out at the resort before that, so I should get going."

"Wow," said Ry. Everett stood up. Ry stood up, too.

"Thanks for flying us over here," he said. "I think it's completely amazing that you built your own airplane. It was nice to meet you. I hope your methane thingy isn't too hard to fix."

He said this while they walked out onto the tiny front porch. He thought he was the only one who was going to be polite, but Yulia came out, too.

"Good luck," said Everett. "Or I guess I should say, 'Bon voyage.'"

They shook hands. Everett said, "C'mon, Loo," patted his leg, and he and Lulu trotted down the steps and out the short piece of sidewalk to the Land Rover.

"See you, Everett," Yulia called out.

Everett waved, got into the vehicle, drove away.

"I can't believe he's flying back the same day," said Ry. "Did you ever fly in that plane?"

"Once," said Yulia. "But it sounds like I had a smoother ride than you did. Was it scary?"

"Only because I don't want to die yet," said Ry.

Yulia laughed.

"Everett didn't seem worried about it, though," said Ry. "So it must have been pretty normal for him. I guess you would get used to it."

"Well, he does it all the time," said Yulia. "It's his hobby. One of his hobbies, anyway. He has a lot of them."

"His methane digester exploded this morning," said Ry.

"His what?" said Yulia. She hadn't heard about that one.

So Ry told her about it. Then, somehow, he found himself telling her about breakfast and the pancakes. He mentioned the argument about the cave.

"You mean the time they were building the wall and one of them put a rock on top that fell and broke something?" asked Yulia.

"Ripped their sleeping bags," said Ry.

"Oh, right," she said. "That's it. They've been arguing about that for twenty years."

"You're kidding," said Ry.

"It's one of their favorite arguments," she said.

Ry looked at her, half smiling, half quizzical. She laughed.

"You've noticed they're both as pigheaded as mules,

right?" She laughed again. "If that makes any sense."

A scraping sound came from above and behind them. They turned and looked up to see Del lifting himself up onto the roofline. He walked along the peak as easily and as sure-footed as if he were walking down a sidewalk.

"You're such a show-off," said Yulia. Del smiled, pleased.

"What are you doing up there?" asked Yulia.

"Checking the connection to your satellite dish," said Del. "I think it might be loose." Arriving at the dish, he stooped on one knee and began his inspection.

"You don't have to fix everything in my house on the first day you're here," said Yulia.

"This is self-interest," said Del. "I want to take a look at the Weather Channel."

"You're going to sail my boat by what the Weather Channel says?" asked Yulia.

"No," said Del. "I was just taking a look, and it didn't work, so . . ." His voice trailed off as he reached down and fiddled with something.

"That might do it," he said. He rose to his feet again, turned, and strolled back to the other end, where there was a tall fence to climb down onto, and disappeared.

Even Ry, who was a guy, and fifteen years old, knew he was watching a love poem. He looked at Yulia. She was still looking up at the roof, though Del wasn't there now. Her expression was hard to read without background information.

It would help to know, for example, that she met Del on her first trip to New England. Her first snow, really. They were both visiting friends, who decided to ski, cross-country, up (and down) a mountain. Yulia had never skied. But how hard could it be? She clipped the borrowed skis onto the borrowed boots. Immediately they slipped out from under her, apparently uncontrollable. She was terrified—of the mountain, of the afternoon ahead—but she didn't want to admit it. Her friends offered advice, but she was flustered. Their advice didn't seem to make sense.

Then Del materialized in front of her. He skied up the mountain backward, facing her. He coaxed her along by telling her stories, telling her she was doing just fine. When they came back down, he put his skis in front of hers, as parents do with children, and guided her down.

It would help to know all the stories like that one.

It would help to know, at the same time, that Del and

Yulia had driven for two hundred miles through Guatemala and Chiapas on a tire with a gash in it, passing by a place where they could have gotten a new one, because Del had his mind set on making it to San Cristóbal before it blew. All of those kinds of stories were in her gaze, too.

How could Ry know any of that?

She turned to him with simple friendliness and said, "We better go see what he's up to."

They went to the marina where Yulia kept her boat, to make sure it ("she") was ready to go, and so that Yulia could show them where everything was. What Ry knew about boats would fit inside a smallish gimbal,* with a lot of room left over, so he trailed along behind Del and Yulia, admiring the hugeness of this one, the sleekness of that one. Some reminded him of sports cars in a way, only the boats were even prettier than that. Others looked like floating RVs. No doubt they were nice to be in, or on; they just didn't look as good. To him. The names of the boats, at least the English ones, were fun to look at, too. He liked the corny ones: *Summer Salt. Vitamin Sea. Can't Fathom It. Freudian Sloop. Get My Drift.*

---

* What—you don't know about boats, either?

The Spanish ones he tried to translate. He could figure out the easy ones: *Suenos. Nada Mucho.* He didn't know what *Chupacabra* was.

The boats that had people on them either had people bustling around doing boat maintenance or people having beers or cocktails. Ry smiled at everyone because it's the universal language and because he was that kind of guy. Some people waved and smiled back, and some did not. Depending on what kind of guys, or gals, they were.

Yulia's boat, when they reached it, was of the sports car type, on the vintage (old) end of the spectrum. Its name was *The Peachy Pie.* She explained to Ry that it was a kind of sailboat that was called a ketch because of where the second mast was. And that, though it was easier with two people, it was a boat one person could manage, if need be.

"Ha!" she said. "Ry on the ketch!" As if that was some kind of joke. "She's a very docile sailor," she went on. "Very forgiving. Because of the rigging."

"Can you say that in English?" Ry asked. Just to keep things from getting too salty.

"She's a peach," said Yulia. "Easy to sail. If you make a mistake, it probably won't kill you. You'll love it."

"Cool," said Ry. Hoping this was true. Because, without

warning, waves of apprehension now rose and collapsed within him. Maybe it was the sailboat, and how oceanic the ocean was looking. Or maybe it was a new thought that was trying to find form in his mind as he walked back down the pier, once again behind Del and Yulia. It seemed as clear as day that they belonged together. He didn't know what had separated them, flung them so far apart, but they were connected by an invisible force field of gravity, history, magnetism, and affection.

The thought that was forming was in fragments. One fragment: There's that old expression, When your only tool is a hammer, everything looks like a nail. Another fragment, also an expression Ry had heard: If you ask surgeons how to fix a health problem, they'll say, "Operate." And one more fragment (this one is a little different): There is the way the seeds of some plants catch on the fur of passing animals to distribute themselves.

So what if Ry's need to reach his family was the shaggy dog that picks up the burr and drops it off in San Juan? What if Del was the surgeon, and going to San Juan was the operation he trusted to solve every problem? What if Ry's journey with Del, from Montana to here, was part of the love poem Del was writing to Yulia when he walked across her roof?

When they had listened to the phone messages in Wisconsin, and Del said, "Let's go find them," it had seemed extreme. But the situation seemed extreme. It had seemed to make sense. It seemed like the right thing to do. Maybe Ry had been temporarily out of his mind. Maybe it was that shower.

Now, back in his right mind, he heard Beth, back in New Pêche, saying, "San Juan. Hmm . . . isn't that where Yulia lives?"

He heard Sharon, in the wilds of Indiana, saying, "Ah, yes, Yulia."

The bizarrity of his situation fell on his shoulders like an iron cloak. The cloak of stupidity. Go find your parents on an island in the Caribbean.

"How stupid am I?" he wondered aloud.

Up ahead of him, Yulia and Del were taking turns making vehement gestures. They stopped and turned to face each other. Both planted fists on their hips. Yulia was animated; Del was immobile, entrenching himself in whatever position it was that he had decided to take. Ry watched them from where he was. He could hear their voices, but not what they were saying. The invisible force field kept him from going any closer.

Two sharp syllables erupted from Yulia. Ry thought he could guess what they were. He watched as she threw up her hands and walked away.

"Come on, Del," Ry said softly, from where he stood. "Just go say you're sorry."

From where he stood, it didn't look like that was going to happen.

# NARUTO

After dinner Ry went into Yulia's den and turned on her computer. He wanted to retreat to some comfortable, familiar, imaginary place. Like the past. His past.

He went to a website that had Naruto clips and watched the bands of anime youth with their giant eyes that in real life would actually be creepy, but on-screen made them look cool, with their spiky hair and their outfits. He looked at some that were just music videos, anime action to songs. Then he looked at some that had stories, usually battles or confrontations where some sinister force had to be faced down. They always knew how to do it.

Yulia came in and took a book from the shelf, probably to bolster her position in the argument she was still having with Del. She stopped to watch, over Ry's shoulder. He wished she would go away, but it was her house, her room, her computer.

"What do you like about that world?" she asked him. "They're so vapid."

"They're cool," he said.

"What's cool about them?" she asked.

"They can jump high. They're ninjas. They have magic powers," he said.

"Okay," she said, but Ry could tell she was unconvinced. She watched for a little longer.

She took her book and left the room. As she walked down the hall, back into the kitchen, he could hear her say, "Okay, listen to this. . . ."

Ry x-ed out of the Naruto site. He sat there looking at the screen, waiting for it to tell him something. Well, you have to ask it something, he said to himself. He thought for a minute, then he typed in "How is this all going to turn out?" and hit Search.

The first 10 of 143 million results were about politics. Voter turnout.

So he tried, "Will everything be okay?"

He watched the forty-four-second "everything will be ok" video on YouTube. It was an animation, with stick figures and blurry blobs. Kind of cool.

He looked at the everythingwillbeok.com website. This was a video, too, apparently an endless (live?) one, of a wacky-waving-inflatable-arm-flailing-tubeman. It had the sound of the tubeman, whipping in the wind. He watched it for about two minutes. It was funny. He found himself smiling.

Easing his way toward the real world, he went to his Facebook page. There was his profile photo, in all his backpacking gear, and his most recent status: "is leaving civilization now."

He scrolled down through his friends' comments. Drivel, mostly. But funny drivel. His inbox had one message. It was from Eric: *You probably won't see this until August if you're at camp, but your last text was weird. And now your phone is turned off. Everything okay?*

Ry typed back: *Some things are kind of messed up right now. But I'm okay. I'll tell you about it later.*

He thought about calling. But Eric couldn't do anything that Ry could think of. Plus, he didn't quite feel up to explaining his current circumstances. It did make him feel better that Eric had noticed something. It made him feel better to say something back.

On Yulia's phone he called the house in Waupatoneka

and retrieved the lone message. The police were going to put the photo of his grandpa on the local TV news, in case anyone had seen him.

How weird was that?

At least he was doing something about it. His parents, he felt sure, would not want to be sailing around from beach to beach while Grandpa Lloyd was who knows where, in who knows what condition. For a few minutes, it all made sense. He knew where his parents were. And he was almost there. So close. He and Del would find them. That would be that, all the what-ifs would drop away.

They weren't far off now, though, the what-ifs. They hovered just outside Ry's field of vision. He knew they were there. He went to Hulu and watched four Simpsons episodes in a row.

## NEURAL PATHWAYS

One hundred thirty-eight miles from the telephone in Waupatoneka, Lloyd sat in a cabin in the woods, near a lake, playing poker with Betty and her sister. Betty thought it would be good exercise for his brain. Create new neural pathways, that sort of thing.

And then, down one of her own neural pathways came the recollection that she had forgotten to call any of the neighbors about the dogs.

"Oh, dear," she said.

"What?" said Ruth.

Betty didn't want to worry Lloyd. She had promised she would call, but there was the reunion, the long night in the woods, the trip to the hospital—she just forgot.

"Oh, nothing," she said. "I remembered something I

said I would do tomorrow." She hoped Ruth wouldn't ask her what.

"Lloyd," she said. "We'll have to drive back to Waupatoneka first thing in the morning, if that's okay." She would tell him when they got there and could do something. Look around. Go to the pound. Whatever you did about dogs.

"Suits me," he said.

## THE MINUTE
## WE GET
## OUR STUFF

A seagull flight (a long seagull flight) from where Ry sat watching Bart and Apu, his mother and father sat talking.

"I think the minute we get our stuff, we should sail this boat back to Annalee, get on a plane, and go home," said his mother. "I'm just not in the mood for this vacation anymore. And it really bothers me that Dad's not answering the phone. What if something happened to him?"

"He never answers the phone," said his dad. "Listen. I know we've had some setbacks. But the odds are with us now. Let's just give it one more chance. Howsabout, when we get all our cards and papers, Monday, we hope, we sail to Saint Jeroen's? It's only two miles away. A really easy sail. We'll do everything easy. Easy, easy, easy."

"I'll think about it," said his mom.

# PART FOUR

## HI-HO

The sea was magnificent. But then there was the deepness and the vastness of it, and the itsy-bitsyness of their boat. It wasn't seasickness Ry felt. This was more akin to panic. He had an intense longing to be on shore, any shore. He would like to be moving from the shore toward the center of a substantial continent. Just think of it like an Imax movie, he said to himself. An Imax movie times four or five or six, a screen in every direction. It didn't help.

He found that he was okay when he concentrated on following Del's instructions. He was okay when he looked at Del, who seemed, as he was in any situation that required physical strength and agility plus mechanical aptitude and that also included unlikely odds, perfectly at ease. Ry was okay when he focused on the sails, the ropes, the varnished wood, the striped cushions that were cheery, though dingy. Anything nearby and a solid.

Eating was calming, too, so he parceled out bites of the sandwiches Yulia had packed, holding each one in his mouth until it had melted to mush and he had to swallow it. He looked at Del, the sails, ropes, wood, cushions, sandwich.

There are people who do this all the time, he told himself.

People drown all the time, too, his self thought to mention.

"Shut up," he said. He said it aloud, and Del, who hadn't said anything, glanced over his shoulder questioningly. Ry shook his head.

Hours went by. Perhaps days, weeks, a lifetime. He began to get a feel for how what they were doing with the sails connected up to how the boat acted with the wind and the watery moguls. In the same way that Pavlov's dogs had gotten a feel for what happened with bells and food. From time to time, he would ask Del a question, or venture a guess as to what their next move would be. He still wasn't letting himself look too far away from the boat, but he settled (relaxed would be too strong a word) into his self-circumscribed sailing experience. Now and again he began to glance outward at the nearest swells, able to see how beautiful they would look from, say, the firmness of a beach.

A seabird of some type floated calmly up and over the rolling foothills of water and down into the valleys. It was a small creature, way smaller than he was himself, yet it was unconcerned with the immensity of what was under it and in every direction for great distances. It was, of course, adapted to this environment. It could float and fly and retrieve meals. Even so, Ry couldn't help admiring what looked like bravado.

He thought of how he had learned to calm his fears on roller coasters by yelling at the top of his lungs. Maybe that explained sea chanties. He tried to think of one. Yo, ho, ho, and a bottle of rum. Hi-ho, hi-ho, it's off to sea we go. Ho, ho, ho, who wouldn't go. Other songs with "ho." Or, It was sad when the great ship went down. That one was about the *Titanic*. Not good to think of now.

In the first part of the sail, they had moved between islands, some closer, some farther off. Del sailed the boat by knowing what islands they were. He knew all of their names and sometimes stories or interesting facts.

There was an island that had been used for bombing practice and there was still live ordnance, so there were places on it that people weren't allowed to go. Oddly enough, that had allowed sea turtles to start to thrive there.

Del pointed at some rocks rising up from the water and told Ry how Sir Francis Drake's men had used them as target practice because the rocks looked to them like the sails of a French warship.

There was an island where they harvested salt.

There was an island called Dead Chest, where the pirate Blackbeard had left fifteen of his men with just a bottle of rum and a sword to punish them. When they tried to swim to the next island, they all drowned. That's where Robert Louis Stevenson got the idea for "Fifteen men on the dead man's chest,/Yo ho ho, and a bottle of rum."

A lot of the stories were about war or pirates. Or war and pirates. There was the salt one, and a place where giant boulders were strewn along the beach like a child's toys. But those weren't stories, really.

Now they were in a stretch with no islands in sight. They were sailing by the compass and by charts. Which meant maps. No GPS; Del had no use for GPS. Besides, Yulia's boat was old and didn't have it. But Del would get them there. It was exactly the kind of thing he was good at.

The boat rocked and rolled. Ry was getting used to the movement. He slid a wrench out of his way that he had awkwardly avoided in some of his quick scrambles along the edge of the boat, and felt he had significantly lessened his chances of flying over the edge. He was wearing a harness that would inflate if he went into the water, but still, he didn't relish the idea of bobbing like a crouton in the sharky broth.

The sun was high now, and the air balmy. Ry attempted to remove his sweatshirt without taking off his harness. He felt foolish, and he didn't like how his hands were trapped inside, unavailable for grabbing. So he took the harness off, pulled off the sweatshirt and flung it quickly behind him, and put the harness back on as fast as he could. Just in time for one of those stretches where it seemed that only the paltry one-hundred-forty pounds of his body, leaning as far back as he dared, was keeping the sailboat from capsizing as it bounded over the water. If this was docile and forgiving, he was glad they weren't sailing a boat that was high-spirited or spiteful.

Del checked the compass, they moved the sails ("Ready about"), and there he was, doing it again, but now on the other side. The place where he had been sitting a moment before was in a steeply diagonal relationship

to where he sat now, and unnervingly close to the water. Don't think, he told himself. Think but then don't think.

And so it went. Back and forth, side to side, tilt this way, tilt that way. The deep tilting was called "heeling." Having a name other than "tipping over" made it seem less dangerous, more like a normal thing that happened all the time, that was okay if it happened. It would be fun in a medium-sized lake. A nice-sized lake with a visible fringe of trees in every direction. A lake where you had to watch out for all the other boats. Where the sound of voices, and the fragrance of grilling and barbecue, sometimes, floated out from the shore.

Del was at the compass again. Ry watched his back, waiting for the "Ready about." But this time Del turned without speaking, and Ry saw on his face an expression that is unnerving to see on your captain's face when you are in such a small sailboat on an immense body of water. It was an expression of bafflement.

Del gazed past Ry into the middle distance, at some hologramic projection of his thoughts. Then it turned out that he was not gazing at spectral thoughts, but at an actual physical presence.

"I wonder what that island is," he said then,

thoughtful, speculative. He looked down at the chart and said, "It's not supposed to be there."

Following Del's gaze, Ry saw a small island in the near distance. It rose, rocky and vegetated, from the sea, and he thought it might be the most beautiful thing he had ever seen. Though he wished it was bigger. He didn't like it that he could see both ends of it at once without moving his head.

A candy-striped lighthouse perched on a rocky ledge. A solitary birthday candle, left in a billion-year-old piece of cake.

"I think we better go see what it is," said Del. "We must have gotten off course. Though I can't think how."

As they drew closer, they saw a man standing on a ledge. He appeared to be watching them. Then he was not there, but it was time to find a place to park the boat. "Park" probably wasn't the right word for it. Land the boat? Beach it?

They sailed along the perimeter, just outside of the breaking waves, searching for an ideal spot. Or an adequate spot. Or a spot that offered the ghost of a prayer of making it ashore in one piece. The slanting light of late afternoon lent a golden glory-glory-hallelujah radiance to flowering trees and bushes, to tantalizing grassy hummocks, to the continuous vertical rock face where the island plunged below the surface to the depths. To be so close, but not able to land . . . what would they do if night fell and they were still circling?

Ry blocked out the image this conjured up, which was a powerful one (black, with heaving, lapping, crashing swells of immense, cold, salty ocean and the boat snapping like a toothpick against invisible-in-the-darkness boulders, and the water so cold, so endless), from his mind, and instead looked at a phalanx of happy goats that came frolicking, fearless of the precipice they danced along, so close to the edge. He might have traded his life as a human for the life of a goat at that moment, but no one made the offer.

Suddenly a shout was heard. Both Ry and Del turned their heads toward it. A man stood—was it the same man?—on an outcropping, waving both arms. When he saw that he had their attention, he pointed. At first they were confused, seeing nothing, but then an almost imperceptible break in the rock opened as they approached, and they saw that the opening led to a hidden cove.

They dropped their sails, and Del started the motor. In they went. As waves entered the narrow passage, the water had to crowd up vertically in the air to fit all its volume in. It was like riding through a washing machine. Once they made it into the cove, though, the waves settled down and rolled in swells toward a pebbly shore.

A modest pier had been constructed there, with what looked to be a fishing boat tied up on one side of it. At Del's instruction, Ry leaped out onto the pier and held the rope that was tossed to him while Del tied another rope to one of the posts.

Ry was giddy at their unexpected luck. He understood that they were not done sailing, but tomorrow was another day. He would have kissed the boards of the pier if he weren't so busy doing what Del was telling him to do. He haffed the chuffs, clipped the ridings, railed the boards, highed the lows, skibed the rampets, harbed the reefs, and cleeted the forths. Which is what sailing talk sounds like if you are not a sailor.

When they had made everything fast, which meant making sure nothing would go anywhere at all, fast or slow, Del said, "Here, grab your sweatshirt. It might cool down later."

He reached for the sweatshirt and picked it up from where Ry had tossed it some hours back. But he didn't hand it to Ry. He clutched it in front of him and looked intently at the place where it had been. The big wrench was lying there, the wrench that Ry had moved out of his way.

"Did you put that there?" he asked Ry.

"Yeah," said Ry, "I kept tripping over it."

Del's face was unreadable. He might have been angry or amused, or puzzling out another mystery, it was hard to say. Ry watched his Adam's apple bob up and down a few times.

He figured it was related to Del's Reverence for Tools, and keeping them where they were supposed to be, but he didn't see why Del had to go all Sphinx-ish on him. It wasn't that big a deal.

"Tell me where it goes and I'll put it away," he said. Whoever had left the wrench where it was in the first place, which by the way wasn't him, hadn't put it away, either.

He climbed back down into the boat and was about to grab the wrench when Del stopped him.

"Wait," Del said. "I just want to show you something. It's pretty important."

He picked up the wrench himself and extended his arm out away from his body. Then he set it back down where it had been.

"Watch the compass," he said, and he moved the wrench away and back again. Ry watched the needle of the mounted compass spin to two o'clock. And he watched it spin back around to point to the approaching wrench. Del set the wrench down and dropped the sweatshirt on top of it.

"Tell me which way's north," he said.

And first, Ry grasped the simple concept that the compass was pointing at the wrench, not at north. And then he grasped the hypothetical version of the idea that they had been sailing on open water, out of sight of land, guided by a compass pointing at a wrench instead of at north. And then he comprehended the concrete, iron, and watery actualization of that idea being carried out in real life. Which had just occurred. And at the same time, he understood that he was the one who had, unwittingly, caused it to happen.

He thought he might throw up.

As his mind swirled, the simple science sank into his brain like lead shot into a whirlpool. As if that weren't enough, he was slammed by the realization of how pissed Del must be. He didn't want to look at him. He looked, instead, at the compass and the sweatshirt for a very long time.

He was aware that Del was moving around the boat. When he lifted his head and opened his mouth to say how sorry he was, and how stupid, what an idiot, Del was climbing out onto the rickety dock.

"Just put it in that cubby over there," said Del.

"I'm sorry I'm such an idiot," said Ry.

"It's my fault as much as yours," said Del. "I forgot to put it away. I left it where you could trip over it."

Then Del was walking down the dock toward the island man, who was coming out onto the dock. Ry saw them meet. He picked up the villainous sweatshirt and climbed out of the boat.

# THE LIGHTHOUSE
# KEEPER
# OF MACETA

*"¡Buenas!"* said the island man to Ry. He spoke warmly.

*"¿Están perdidos, o son estupidos, o locos?"*

"Do you speak Spanish?" Del asked. "I think I understood 'good' and 'stupid.'"

"I take it in school," said Ry. "He wants to know if we are lost, stupid, or crazy."

"Tell him, All three," said Del. "All three, and even more."

*"Todos los tres, y mas,"* said Ry. His Spanish was not that smooth. But it was better than nothing. The island man laughed.

*"¿Saben, dónde están?"* he asked.

*"No,"* said Ry. *"No se."*

*"¿Tienen un mapa?" preguntó el hombre de la isla.*

"He wants to know if we have a map," said Ry.

"I'll get it," said Del. "Ask him how far it is to St. Jude's." He trotted back to the boat to retrieve the map and back while Ry tried to remember how to phrase the question.

"¿Como . . . cuánto distancio hay a St. Jude's?"

"¿No tienen GPS?"

"No, no GPS."

"Ah, OK," dijo el hombre. "Por cierto, soy Alejandro."

Aha! An easy one!

"Mucho gusto," dijo Ry, and shook Alejandro's mano. "Me llamo Ry; y se llama Del. Somos de los Estados Unidos." He hoped Alejandro would ask him how old he was, if he had any brothers and sisters, and what sports he liked. He could say all of those things.

"¡No me digan!" dijo Alejandro. "¿Cual fue mi primera pista?" This meant, No kidding, what was my first clue? Though Ry didn't get it.

Alejandro took one side of the map Del had brought over and pulled it open.

"Esto se llama St. Jeroen. Nosotros estamos aquí— esta isla se llama 'Maceta,' la ultima isla antes de llegar al océano, el Atlántico. Tienen suerte que pararon aquí. El mar es enorme y África está muy lejos."

Roughly: This island is called Maceta ("flowerpot").

You are lucky you stopped here. It's the last island before the Atlantic. It's quite a large ocean—a long way to Africa.

"*¿La ultima isla?*" asked Ry.

"*Sí,*" *dijo Alejandro.*

"*¿Antes de Africa?*" asked Ry.

"*Sí.*"

*Ry miró el mapa. Miró* at the dot Alejandro had pointed to. He pondered the wrench, the compass, and the finite-but-not-finite-enough Atlantic. He was pretty sure Del got the picture, but he felt compelled to say it anyway.

"We could have died," he said. "We could have kept going out into the ocean and never landed."

"But we didn't," said Del. "That's what makes it a happy story instead of a sad story."

He said it in a lighthearted, singsong way, as if he were speaking to a child.

"*¡Ven conmigo!*" *dijo Alejandro. "Les indicaré dónde está su isla.*"

Come with me. I'll show you where your island is.

He gestured for them to follow.

# ISLANDS COME,
# ISLANDS GO

They climbed a path that traversed the face of the hillside, tacking sharply to the left and the right through profusions of trees and bushes and flowers to negotiate its steepness. Tiny lizards darted and paused. Creatures that seemed something between a squirrel and a prairie dog rose up out of shrubbery to watch them pass. Goats looked out at them through horizontal pupils but did not stop munching.

The path was wide enough for two of the three to walk abreast. It was only dirt, but it had been carved out and graded with some care. At the top of it, a cart waited. They squeezed past it into a generous clearing, a taming of the undergrowth. As well as the overgrowth.

A low stone wall meandered around the free-form perimeter. At one end a rounded lobe of the clearing held a garden. The striped lighthouse towered from the other end. Midway between the two sat a whitewashed cottage with a red tile roof. In front of it, something roasted on a spit over a fire. Untroubled chickens, reddish brown and white and black-and-white ones, trolled picturesquely upon the green for bugs and worms, scratching and dipping, throughout the territory.

Alejandro led them over to the lighthouse, where they ascended a stairway carved into one of the boulders at its base. From there, they had an unobstructed view of . . . water and air. Sea and sky. It was a panorama that gave new meaning to the word *island*. Or the words *the ends of the earth*. They were standing on one of those ends.

Then Alejandro pointed and said, *"¡Miren! ¡Allí!"* Look, there. They *miraron* and *vieron otra isla*. Another island. A little bump rising from the sea.

Now Alejandro took the map from Del and opened it again. He pointed and used kindergarten-level words Ry could mostly understand, to show and tell them that the island they were looking for was on the other side of the island they could see.

*"Ya casi están allí,"* he said. You are almost there.

"How far?" asked Del. "Ask him how long it will take us."

*"¿Cuánto tiempo por ir? ¿Cuántos horas?"* asked Ry. How many time to go? How much hours?

*"Esta noche es demasiado tarde, pero mañana, al medio dia. Con buena suerte y viento fuerte,"* dijo Alejandro. It's too late tonight. But tomorrow, by lunchtime. With luck and good wind.

*"¿No lo podemos hoy? ¿Seguro?"* asked Ry. Not today? Sure? He could see that the sun was falling toward the horizon. And to be honest, he had no desire to jump back into the boat.

*"¿Conocen bien las estrellas?"* dijo Alejandro. How well do you know the stars? And, *"Un sitio para descansar por una noche es preferible a uno permanente."* A temporary resting place is better than a permanent one.

Of which Ry understood "is better than" and "permanent." It gave him the gist.

*"¿Si están tan apurados, por qué viajan en velero?"* preguntó Alejandro. If you are in a hurry, why are you in a sailboat? And, *"La noche no será larga. ¿Que hay tan importante allá?"* The night is not long. What is so important there?

It was a reasonable question. Ry wasn't sure his Spanish was up to it, so he just shrugged. But later, he tried to answer it as they sat chewing on roasted meat of some kind. Which was not that bad. Actually, really good.

"My grandfather is lost. In the United States. My mother and father are here on a boat, or an island. We look for them.

"My grandfather's head . . ." He couldn't remember how to say that something *might* be happening. Or might have already happened.

"Danger," he said. "We need to find him. My parents need . . . to know. To help."

"*¿Esta seguro que ellos estan por St. Jude's?*" Are you sure they are on St. Jude's?

Yes. I think that. I hope it.

The thing was, his days were getting mixed up now. What day it was, which day his parents had said they were leaving. He was pretty sure it was tomorrow that was the now-or-why-bother day.

# THE
# CRUMBLING
# CUPCAKE

"*¿Solamente usted vive aquí?*" asked Ry. "*¿En esta isla?*" Only you here? In this island?

The three of them sat on the porch of the little cottage, around a table which held the detritus of their meal. Ry was the interpreter. Piecing together a conversation with his level of Spanish skills was like building a bridge out of toothpicks and gumdrops. You wouldn't want to put a lot of weight on it—yourself, for example—but it took your mind off your worries.

"*Sólo yo y las ardillas de tierra,*" said Alejandro. Only me and the burrowing squirrels.

Ry didn't know the words for burrowing squirrels. "*¿Ardillas de tierra?*" he repeated. "*¿Que son esas?*"

Alejandro smiled. He held up a finger, then the palm of his hand, indicating that they should wait *uno momento*, then disappeared into the house. He returned with a book, a notebook, and a pen. Ry and Del stacked the dirty dishes and pushed them aside to make a space on the table.

Alejandro opened the book to a photograph. Ry and Del recognized the squirrel/prairie dog they had seen so many of as they climbed up the hill. Through words, sketchy diagrams, and hand gestures, Alejandro told them that the *animalitos* had been brought to the island from another land, long ago. They were brought by a man who intended to raise them as livestock. As a gourmet delicacy. They were very tasty. As you already know, he added. Then some of them escaped. It was a jailbreak; they escaped by digging tunnels. Burrows. Because that was the kind of animals they were, burrowing animals. They started burrowing all over the island. It was their nature.

Part of the island was rock, solid, and they couldn't burrow through that. But after a while, there were so many of them burrowing through the softer parts that whole chunks of the island became unstable and fell right off, into the sea.

The island used to be bigger, Alejandro said. *"Antes era más grande."* People had lived here, then. Ry wondered what would happen when the squirrels ran out of dirt. Alejandro thought maybe they would learn to swim and take over the ocean, too. Not really, he said. But when there were so many, they reminded you of *cucarachas*. Cockroaches. Pests.

"Wow," said Ry. *"¡Caramba!"*

*"Sí,"* said Alejandro.

Allowing for the possibility that he had completely misunderstood or that Alejandro had just been alone on the island too long (though he seemed more rational and sane than Ry thought he himself would be in that circumstance), it was an interesting story. Creepy. In the crawly sense.

Trying to fall asleep on yet another sofa—this one was not much more than thin cushions on a bench— Ry imagined the island crumbling out from under them in the night. He cast back earlier into the day for a more sleep-friendly image. He came up with the boat. The little boat tipping and tilting in the big ocean. The wrench and the compass. He cast back further. The homemade airplane. Nothing much in recent history was soothing.

"It's cool that you know some Spanish." Del's voice came from just a few feet away. He was bedded down, or up, in a hammock. "My brain can barely manage English."

"Your brain does lots of other things, though," said Ry. "You're like the ninja cowboy fix-it man." He knew somehow that Del was smiling in the dark. So he went on. "You're like, 'Howdy, ma'am, do you have any broken appliances? Excuse me while I rewire your toaster quick-a-minute.' Zipzapzoop, blow on your fingers, walk into the sunset. 'Oh, you need a ride to the other side of the world? I was just going there.'"

A stray moonbeam found the way through a window and fell in a faint square on the faded carpet, leaving the darkness around it blacker and more velvety. Soft, mild air moved almost imperceptibly in and out of the room. With it floated the gentle traces of ocean salt, flower and vegetation scents, earthy essences, campfire smoke molecules, lingering aromas of roasted foods, effable evidence of human exertion (meaning sweat), all dissolved in great quantities of fresh pure washed air to make a soporific mélange. Sleep Potion Number Nine.

The next island was visible from here. That is, it would be, come morning. There was only one more island after that. Del would get them there. It would all work out.

"And how do you even know how to sail a sailboat?"

Ry mumbled into the lullaby of stillness close by and breakers harmonizing rhythmically down below. "You live in Montana. How do you know about the rocks that look like a French warship?"

His words drifted invisibly away from him like seed fluff on the night air. There was no answer from Del. Ry wouldn't have heard it anyway.

# WHILE HE SLEPT
# AND AFTER HE WOKE

Ry slept profoundly. No dreams could find their way into the black velvet canyons of his sleep. He was physically exhausted, and his mind and his emotions threw in the towel, too. For several hours the lights were out; all was silent. He did keep breathing. He had a pulse. His heart pumped blood through his veins; his organs functioned at a basic level. That was pretty much it.

But wait—a dim light, a soft humming was coming from somewhere. Up in the attic. Brain cells were still sifting through the events of the day and rearranging themselves in light of what had happened. They were looking for ways to organize the new information. They were talking it around and building tentative synapses. Networking.

His muscles were also reviewing their performance.

They were blaming everything on the head. This was all stuff they could do. Get over yourself, they said. Lead, follow, or get out of the way. They were prodding. They knew they could not do it alone.

I'm working on it, said Ry's mind.

At what, the speed of mulch? taunted the muscles.

Which is to say, the speed of geniuses since the dawn of time, said the brain, unperturbed. Go flex yourself.

All of these messages traveled osmotically, chemically, through processes but dimly understood, and only by statistically microscopic numbers of humans. They worked on their separate but intertwined tasks through the night. The conclusion they reached was provisional. Ry woke up feeling the uncertainty of the truce, though to himself he just said, I don't want to get in that boat again. But it's the only way out. Don't want to. Only way. Back and forth it went.

After a breakfast abundant with eggs, they made their way down the jackknife turns of the trail. There was the boat; there was the water. Still liquid, still roiling, still mighty.

The de-haffing of the chuffs, the unclipping of the ridings, the lowing of the highs, and so forth to the cleats.

Or rather, the removal of the sail covers, the checking

of the bilges, the eyeballing of the rigging.

Suddenly Ry seemed to know what the words meant. Maybe the part of his brain that had been activated by trying to speak Spanish was also working on speaking sailing. He was sailing in tongues.

Del made him put sunblock on, then they waved *adios* to Alejandro, and motored through the slim tumultuous passage out to the open sea.

Del called out to Ry to hoist the mizzen, and he did so.

Del called out to Ry to hoist the mainsail, and he did.

Del called out to Ry to belay the halyard to the cleat on the mast, and he was already doing it. They looked at each other and laughed.

The first island was in sight and they were headed for it. As they drew closer, the second island, *the* island, crept out from behind the first. The boat danced over the swells. They had a steady breeze. The sails hauled them along, the water sparkled around them, a million diamonds of light skittering over the surface. Ry could not think of anything he had ever done that felt better than this. Not that he was trying to. He wasn't thinking at all, about anything, except wind, sails, water, sun.

A couple of times, when the sails were set and all

they had to do was lean back and be exhilarated, inner bits of Ry and Del that were usually snugged in tight somewhere loosened up and leaked out. Floated out.

Ry told Del how once, as a little kid, he had stopped to tie his shoe while his family walked from their car to a restaurant. When he had tied it, he stood up and ran after them. He grabbed his father's hand and started talking away, until he looked up and saw that it wasn't his father. Same build, same kind of coat, total stranger. A nice-enough stranger.

When Ry saw that it wasn't his father, he burst into tears. His parents by now had turned to look for him, and he saw them and ran to them and buried his face in his mother's coat. As the stranger walked by he said pleasantly, "I thought I had a little boy for a minute there." All three grownups laughed. Ry was mortified. He wouldn't even look at the guy.

Ry hadn't thought of this for a long time, and it surprised him when it came to mind.

Del said he wished he hadn't argued with Yulia.

"I was really determined not to," he said.

"You should just say you're sorry," said Ry. "Say you were wrong."

"What if I don't think I was wrong?" said Del.

"Well, how important was it, whatever you were arguing about?" asked Ry.

"Not that important," said Del. "But I wasn't wrong."

Ry said, "All you have to do is say you're sorry, then. Or you can say you were wrong, but leave out part. Like, maybe the whole sentence would be, 'There may have been times in my life when *I was wrong*; I'm not saying this was one of them.' Or you could say, 'I could be wrong,' and leave out the 'but I doubt it' part."

Del said, "That seems a little dishonest."

Ry said, "Not as long as you really mean the part you say aloud. 'I'm sorry. I could be wrong.' Or just, 'I could be wrong.' Then at least the person knows it's not completely pointless to keep talking to you.

"Didn't you ever go to preschool?" he asked Del.

"No," said Del. "They didn't have preschool back then. We had to go right out and forage for nuts and berries."

After a time they were passing fairly close to the first island. This one was large, and populated. Boxy houses that looked small from out here, but probably weren't, were sprinkled over the hillsides, nestled in the foliage. Farther along, a flock of buildings and boats formed a harbor town.

**2 9 5**

Ry didn't notice the windmill until Del pointed it out to him. Del said it was hundreds of years old. It had been taken apart in the Netherlands, brought here in pieces, and put meticulously back together. This was a Dutch island, owned and operated by the Dutch. It was called St. Jeroen. Del said he had always wanted to take a look at the windmill. He was a big fan of windmills.

"And here we are," he said. "So close." He squinted toward the windmill.

"I wonder if they're taking care of it," he said. "I wonder if they're even using it, or if it's just there for tourists to look at and take pictures of."

The way he said this made Ry smile. It was as if he were talking about an animal, a noble old animal forced to wear a silly costume and do tricks in a traveling circus.

"Do you want to go check on it?" he asked. "Make sure it's okay?"

"Do you mind?" Del said quickly. "I think we have plenty of time. It's still pretty early. It wouldn't take very long. I'm just curious. I'd like to take a look at it, up close."

Ry thought he knew what was coming next, so he decided to say it himself.

"It would be stupid to pass it by when we're so close," he said. "It wouldn't feel right."

"That's how I feel, too," said Del.

"But we won't stay very long, right?" asked Ry.

"Not long at all," said Del. "A quick look and we're back on our way."

"Okay," said Ry. "Let's go."

As they headed for shore, he yelled to Del, "If it needs to be fixed, you have to come back after we find my mom and dad."

# THE WINDMILL

The main harbor was behind them. They could have made a U-ey and headed for it, but they spied a boat emerging from another inlet, closer to hand, and decided to go there. This seemed to be nearer the windmill anyway. No way to tell yet if the windmill was milling anything, but the blades were spinning merrily around. Glancing to the south, Ry saw the island of St. Jude's. It was close enough that he could make out the movement of a tiny car climbing a steep tiny road that traversed the face of the mountain rising behind the port. It was unbelievable. They were almost there. He felt his blood quicken and more than a mild astonishment: they had actually done this. But there was no time to bask yet. They had swells to slice. They had rollers to romp over, spray to be soaked by.

"Be right there, Mom," he said over his shoulder at the clump of verdant volcano tips. He turned back to St. Jeroen's. The inlet they entered looked like paradise. Two other boats were anchored in the azure waters off the white sand beach. Del and Ry dropped anchor, too. They lowered themselves into the dinghy and paddled in.

The windmill, when they reached it, was a tourist attraction, but not too crowded. There was a guide dressed in a Dutch costume, but his hair was in dreads so he didn't look that authentically Dutch. He demonstrated how flour was made between some grindstones, then he would sell people a bag of it if they wanted one.

Del asked several questions, but it was clear the Dutch miller was not a real miller, either, because he didn't know most of the answers. He was just someone getting paid probably not much to dress up in his outfit and be friendly. Del kept asking questions, because he was interested and curious, but when he started talking about the industrial revolution and alternative energy, the miller looked at him, amused, and said, "The wind blows, the wheels turn, I put the flour into a sack. Do you want some?"

So Del and Ry went back outside while the handful of other people lined up to buy paper sacks of flour.

Ry wandered around the base of the windmill while Del was completing his observations. The stone foundation it rested on looked fairly ancient, and he wondered if that, too, had been brought from the Netherlands, or if the St. Jeroenians had built that themselves. On the back side, he looked up at the cranking arms that translated the spinning of the blades into the turning of the grindstones. Okay, he thought, that makes sense. I get it. Humans were pretty brilliant, really, to think up stuff like this. Of course, it had taken several dozen eons to get to the windmill. Still, he was glad someone had done it. Because of how one thing leads to another. First the windmill, then just an epoch or so later, the airplane propeller. Though he couldn't say that was currently his favorite invention. That would be the pillow-top mattress.

A movement caught his eye. He followed it and saw that Del was climbing up the side of the windmill.

"What are you doing?" he called out. Meaning, Why are you doing it? He flashed on what Everett had said about going rock climbing with Del. "When the rope is attached to Del," he had said, "I tend to think of it more as a leash."

Del hauled himself along the braces under the

decking, then pulled himself up and over the railing onto the deck.

"It's my favorite thing to do on windmills," he said over his shoulder. He jumped up onto the railing and walked along on it with his arms out to his sides, like a tightrope walker. It was kind of funny: Del didn't want the windmill to be forced to perform circus tricks, but he didn't mind doing them himself. Now he grabbed onto one of the giant blades as it rose swiftly beside him. He was lifted into the air. The part he grabbed was a crossbar of wooden latticework. He shifted the position of his hands once or twice as he rode up and around to maintain a comfortable angle, a good grip.

He did it the way he did everything, as if he did this every day. As if it were the easiest thing in the world. As if any sane person would do the same.

He hung gracefully from the turning blade by one arm as he turned to step lightly back onto the railing when it came within reach.

The railing was wooden and it was old. Maybe not hundreds of years old, maybe it had been replaced at some point, but not lately. The expression on Del's face as it gave way beneath him was one of surprise.

His eyes met Ry's as if to say, "What the heck? What

just happened?" His arms and legs went slowly spinning in a weird echo of the blades still spinning behind him, but in the opposite direction. As he fell through the air he began the movement of pulling into a tuck, but this was a trick he hadn't practiced. The timing was off. He met the Earth before he was ready.

For his part, Ry watched Del fall as if he were the pitch, the shuttlecock, the ball in some sport Ry had never learned how to play. What was he supposed to do here? Catch him? Before he could figure it out, there was, almost all at once, the thud of Del reaching the ground and the snapping sound of cracking bones. And Del lay there, his limbs all wrong to his body.

Ry ran and knelt beside him. Del's eyes fluttered open and shut, and then stayed shut. Ry put his fingertips to the place on the neck where you can feel a pulse. Without opening his eyes, Del said, "I'm not dead, but I think I might need a doctor." His voice vibrated in Ry's fingertips. Ry pulled his hand away, startled. Then someone else's fingertips were on Del's throat, a woman's. Ry looked up to see one of the tourist ladies kneeling on Del's other side. The whole group of tourists huddled a few yards off, along with the miller, each one holding a brown paper bag. It was like an advertisement for brown paper bags.

Except that with the expressions on their faces, it was more like a warning against brown paper bags.

Ry glanced down and saw something protruding from the skin on Del's leg. He realized it was Del's bone. Everything sort of disappeared then and went black, until he felt the doctor's warm hand on his cheek, turning his head for him. Her voice said, "Just look at his face for now." So he did.

The doctor said, "Is he your father?"

Still looking at Del's face, Ry wondered if he only imagined a smile moving through it.

"No," said Ry. "He's my friend."

When the ambulance arrived, it was a taxi, a minibus of a manufacture Ry hadn't seen before. The driver jumped out and peeled off the magnetic TAXI signs on each side. He replaced them with signs that said AMBULANCE, and then it was an ambulance. There was even a light on the roof.

The driver hurried over with a bag. Ry was apprehensive, but the guy was not inept. He took one look, then went back to the minibus and returned with a human-sized board with straps on it. Somehow he and the doctor and Ry gently maneuvered Del onto the board without altering his arrangement too much and secured him there. Ry and the driver carried him over to the minibus and loaded him in through a door in the back, sliding him along the aisle between the seats.

The doctor rode along to the hospital. The road was not smooth. With every bump, Ry and the doctor (and Del, no doubt) winced. They looked back and down at Del. His eyes were still closed.

The doctor said to Ry, "Does he often do things like that?"

"Yeah," said Ry. "He kind of does. But I've never seen him fall before."

"The wood was rotten," she said.

Ry was grateful that she didn't say it was a stupid thing to do. She just said her name was Shirley, and that Del would be okay. Eventually.

"He'll be laid up for a while, though," she said. "No wing-walking for a few months."

Bump. Ba-da-bump.

# IN THE HOSPITAL

The hospital was a low building of whitewashed cement. The driver had been talking on his phone to the staff there, so at the instant they pulled under the drive-through carport, the doors opened and two people emerged with a gurney.

Shirley was off the bus in a flash to meet them behind the minibus. She spoke with them while they hauled Del back out. Ry could hear her American English and their island-accented English going back and forth through the opened door. They all spoke quickly, but softly and calmly; more routine than urgent, but also more urgent than routine. Someone must have made a joke while Ry was coming around back, and they all laughed.

Then Del was rolled inside and the doors closed.

Shirley took Ry by the arm and they went inside, too.

There were forms to fill out. Information was needed. Ry and Shirley did the best they could with what they could find in Del's wallet, brought to them after his pants were cut away from his off-kilter limbs.

"KerHodie," said Shirley, reading Del's last name from his driver's license. "What is that, Dutch?"

"I don't know," said Ry. "I think so."

"Sounds Dutch," mused Shirley. "Looks Dutch. He looks Dutch. But maybe it's just because I'm on this Dutch island. Maybe it's just that windmill."

When they had finished with the forms, Shirley turned to Ry and asked, "Is your family nearby?"

It seemed like a trick question.

"Yeah, they are," said Ry. "Why?"

"Well, maybe you should call them," said Shirley. "I need to get back to my own family."

"Oh, right," said Ry. "I will. You should go—I mean, thank you for coming here. It really helped a lot. I wouldn't have known what to say. What to do."

"I'm sure you would have figured it all out," she said. "But it's easy for me, it's what I do, so I'm glad to help. Well, take care, then."

They shook hands and said good-bye, then Shirley

was off, down the hall, around the corner. Maybe the ambulance became a taxi again. Ry stood in the hallway, irresolute.

Absentmindedly, he flipped open Del's wallet, which he was still holding. Del's face looked out through a scratched acetate window. There was a folded piece of paper sticking out that Shirley had opened, glanced at, then refolded and replaced in one of the credit card slots. Ry took it out now and opened it up. He had seen it before, but it was different now. It was the poem he had found in the typewriter that first morning he woke up in Del's house. There was the blob of Wite-Out he had applied, trying to conceal his nosiness.

But the poem had been revised. The revisions were handwritten, in pencil and in pen. The poem wasn't about interplanetary gravity at all. It was about Yulia. Yulia and Del. A title, "For Yulia," had been written at the top, in blue ballpoint:

*For Yulia*

Try as I might,
I can't escape your gravity.
My orbit is elliptical:

**3 0 7**

I fling myself far and I think I'm free.

Who am I kidding?

Invisible forces, and visible ones, come into play:

A stranger comes to town, someone goes on a trip.

Leaving and staying away

Is as easy as falling off the face of the Earth,

But who would want to,

Anyway?

A stranger comes to town, someone goes on a trip. That would be me, Ry thought. The invisible force.

The hospital was small. It didn't take long to find Del. He was on a bed, and a nurse was hooking him up to an IV bottle. Del, despite being in obvious pain, watched her closely. Like next time he might just go ahead and do this part himself and he needed to know how. When he saw Ry, he seemed relieved.

"Call Yulia," he said, "and tell her where I am."

"Do you know her number?" asked Ry. "I don't even know her last name, to try to look her up."

Del rattled off the number as if it was one long word. "Tell her what happened," he said, "and ask her to come."

"Wait a minute," said Ry, searching around for a

pen. He found one on the clipboard on Del's bed. "Okay, what?"

Del said it again and Ry wrote it on the back of his hand.

"Tell her I said I could be wrong," Del said. "And I'm sorry. And then you should go to Saint Jude's and find your mom and dad. You need to get there today."

"How am I supposed to do that?" asked Ry. "I can't sail the boat by myself. And I can't just leave you here."

"Yulia will come," said Del. "She might not stay, but she'll come."

"Okay," said Ry.

"I was wrong about the wood on that railing," said Del. "I should have noticed that."

"Everyone makes mistakes," said Ry.

"That's what I'm saying," said Del. "I was also wrong about the pancakes. Everett was right. You don't go by the thermostat. Any idiot knows that."

"What?" said Ry.

"And I was wrong about opera music. I thought I hated it, but now I don't mind it so much every now and then. In small doses. Very small."

"Oh," said Ry. "I get it. You can say you were wrong. That's great, Del."

"Right," said Del. "I was wrong about taking the air pollution control stuff out of cars, too. It's pretty important to leave it in there."

"Okay," said Ry. "You can stop now."

"I was wrong about being right," said Del. The expression on his face had relaxed to a goofy half grin. The medications dripping into Del's bloodstream must be taking effect.

"I was right about being left," said Del. He was still smiling, but his eyes were falling shut in fluttering stages. His voice was a loopy drawling singsong.

"I was left about . . . " His voice trailed off; his head lolled gently to one side. Ry thought he was out. Then Del's eyes opened and he said in a clear, normal voice, " . . . about three years ago, I think."

His eyes were not open when he said the last words Ry heard him say that day. Which were, "Her last name is KerHodie."

It wasn't until the nurse came back into the room that Ry realized his mouth was open. He closed his mouth and smiled at her, a slight courtesy smile that his face did out of habit. Then he walked out, thinking.

Ry called Yulia. He asked the hospital people if he could call Del's family, and they let him.

His mind was so busy running through all the things he might say that it took him by surprise when he heard Yulia's actual voice, answering her phone.

"Yulia!" he said as if he had met her unexpectedly, on the street.

"Yes?" she said, not recognizing his voice, but recognizing that he was a "yes" person, not a "sí" person.

The conversation was short. Of course she would come.

"He said to tell you he was sorry," said Ry. "And that he was wrong."

"He said he was wrong?"

"Well—he said he could be wrong."

Yulia laughed. "I guess that's a start, isn't it?" she said. She said she'd see him that afternoon, maybe not till evening or night, depending on what she could work out.

"Okay," said Ry. "See you then."

Although he wouldn't see her then, he thought, or maybe ever. He hung up the phone and handed it back to the person behind the desk.

Putting one foot in front of the other, he walked down the corridor, pausing only to scarf a couple of uneaten rolls from a rack of dinner trays. He jammed two more in his pockets and walked through the reception area and out the front door. Where he hesitated, just briefly, in the shade of the carport drive-through, squinting out into the brightness that bathed the day. Then, putting one foot in front of the other, he walked in the direction of the windmill and the cove where the boat was anchored. He didn't know exactly where it was, but this was an island. If he stayed near the shore, how lost could he get?

# NEXT

The forested old lava cones, the mountains of St. Jude's, seemed so close. Not so close that Ry could see his father half walking, half running out to the end of a dock, waving what looked like paper packets, manila envelopes maybe, in the air. But from time to time, a gap in the foliage allowed him a glimpse of the buildings of the port town. He remembered from the lighthouse keeper's map that the town was called Finisterre.

If he could see the buildings, how far could it be? Far enough to swallow up any sound, even someone shouting, even two people shouting what sounded like, "All right! Yes! Let's go!" But he could feel the pull of it, almost like a magnet, or like gravity. He had to get there. He had to do it today.

Magical powers would be helpful; flying, or at least really long jumping.

Against the odds, Ry recognized something about a road that branched off to his right. And, against the odds, it led to the idyllic cove where the *Peachy Pie* floated, bobbing gently on her tether. He pulled the dinner rolls from his pockets and sat in the white sand, in the shade of a bevy of palms, chewing. He wished he had a little more spit to help with the swallowing, or something wet to wash them down with. There were some bottles of water out on the *Peachy Pie*, but he hadn't screwed up his nerve to go out there yet. He waited for the eating of the bread to help with that, but it wasn't happening. He might have to fake the courage part.

He paddled the Zodiac, the dinghy, out to the boat, and climbed up into it. Okay. Here he was. He found the water and took a swig.

Yulia had said one person could sail the boat alone, if need be. "You'll love it," she had said. And he had loved it, not right away, not yesterday, but this morning. That was only, like, a hundred years ago now.

But as Ry moved around the boat, checking lines,

reminding himself of how everything worked, he realized that the person who could sail this boat alone was not him. Who was he kidding? Someday he might be that person, but today wasn't that day. He could help sail a boat, but he wasn't ready to do it alone, not on the open water. The very deep, very open water. There was courage, and then there was stupidity. He sat on the foredeck and gazed unseeing at the twin peaks of St. Jude's. What would happen if he didn't get there today?

His mother and father would move on; he would not know where. Eventually, though, they would go home. He would call them then, from Yulia's, where he would sleep on the couch. After the two of them sailed her boat back to San Juan. They would fly Del there somehow. Maybe Everett would help with that. Then Ry and Yulia would visit Del in the hospital, or he would be at Yulia's, recuperating. In the meantime, though, his grandfather was on the loose with a malfunctioning head. And the dogs—he tried to tell himself the dogs would be okay, but he couldn't help picturing grisly scenarios. Gristley scenarios.

And, what would happen if he did get to St. Jude's, and if he did find his parents? What could they do about any of it? Ry didn't know anymore.

"I think they should know about Grandpa Lloyd, though," he said aloud. If he was found, he would need to be taken care of. Or . . .

"They need to know, either way," he said.

"I wish there was a ferry," he said.

There was a ferry, but he didn't know that, let alone where it was. If there is a ferry and you don't know it, can it still get you to the next island? No.

He was roused from this reverie by movement in front of him. One of the other sailboats was moving, motoring toward the mouth of the cove. Ry waved.

"Hi," he called out.

"Hey, mate," answered the man in the other boat. He sounded Australian. Austrylian. Ry watched the boat head for the sea. The sails went up. Gently, they caught the breeze. Serenely, mildly, the boat eased south.

"Look," it whispered back to Ry. "It's easy."

The winds did appear to be calm. The *Peachy Pie* was a docile sailor, a forgiving boat. He would just go outside the cove. If the wind and the water were too big, he could scoot back in.

Ry put on his harness and clipped it to a tether. He raised the mizzen and sheeted it in tight, the way Del had showed him. He motored the *Peachy Pie* slowly forward till she was directly over the anchor. He trotted up to the windlass and winched the anchor up, then ran back to the cockpit and put the engine in gear. So far, so good.

Motoring out of the cove, he went over in his mind what he had to do next. On reaching the open water, he was relieved to find that the winds really were mild. He would have to put up the biggest jib just to get anywhere.

Here is where an experienced sailor might say, Why didn't he just motor the whole way? Why put up the sails at all? It's not that far. The omniscient narrator does not, in this case, know everything. The best I can come up with is, It didn't occur to him. They had never done it that way before, and he was trying to do everything just as he had been taught. That was challenging enough in itself, without getting creative.

Doing the tasks in a methodical way was calming. As Ry raised the sails, his confidence grew. It was a calm day; it was just the one little stretch of water. It could work. If he had looked up from his tasks, he might have seen the whitecaps in the distance. He might have seen how as the Austrylian's boat moved clear of the headland, out of the shelter of the island, it caught the winds blowing from the open ocean and went roaring across the water. The Austrylian was hollering "Wahoo!" and hanging on for dear life. And that was after he lowered his mainsail halfway.

But Ry didn't look up, so he didn't see that. He got the sails raised and secured and moved steadily, even tranquilly, along. An experienced sailor might find this slowness boring, but Ry was not experienced, so he felt exhilarated. He felt lucky that he was able to pull this off.

Lucky, lucky, lucky: the *Peachy Pie* cleared the headland. Her big sails were filled to bursting with the mighty ocean air funneling between the islands. She screamed along, as manageable as an unpinched balloon. Along with the noise of the wind and the sloshing and slapping of water, Ry could hear the sounds of stuff slamming around below deck. It was a bad sound. But he couldn't worry about it. He knew now that he had too much sail up, and he struggled to wrestle down the big jib.

But before he could do so, a rogue gust of wind, an

invisible fist of air, pushed the boat over onto her side, like a child knocking over a bathtub toy. Ry lost his footing. He hung briefly in the air, an astronaut taking a space stroll at the end of a lifeline. And then he was entering the water. An aquanaut, now.

## IN THE DRINK

$D$el was wrong about one more thing. It wasn't that hard to fall off the face of the Earth, if you included "under" as one of the ways you could do it. Three-quarters of Ry was already below, dangling from the life-jacketed top of him like the tentacles of a jellyfish. His harness inflated as he went under, lifting his top one-quarter back to the surface. A jellyfish. Or a lily pad.

The *Peachy Pie* lay on her side, a giant wounded seabird, rising and falling. Water was flooding the cockpit. She would fill up and then sink.

The Zodiac dinghy was still right side up, but it would be dragged under when the *Peachy Pie* went down. Unless Ry could get there and free it. He moved his arms and legs in swimming motions that had always worked well in pools and lakes. Here in the ocean they didn't seem to be doing anything at all. He had no other ideas, though, so he kept trying.

He could see the big boat going lower. The place where the Zodiac's rope was tied to it was underwater, but he could still untie it at the dinghy end. If he could get there.

In a flash of brilliance, Ry remembered that he also was tethered to the sinking boat. That was a bad thing, but he used the tether to haul himself close, then worked his way along the face of the deck to the stern. Once there, he set himself free, then lunged for the rope that tethered the dinghy.

The life jacket itself was a mixed blessing. It kept you afloat, a benefit that was hard to argue with, but doing anything else was next to impossible. Like grabbing a submerged rope. Or swimming toward a dinghy. There was no doubt a technique for it. After a long and considered analysis—about 1.5 seconds—of what might work best, Ry opted for desperate thrashing.

Okay—no.

But he had moved closer, close enough that when he stopped thrashing, thinking to try something else, the rope floated up between his legs. It brushed his calf and instinctively he squeezed his legs together. When the rope stayed there, didn't swim away, didn't move, Ry lifted his knees, reached down and felt it, and knew it was the rope. He drew himself to the dinghy.

Getting on top of it would be another feat of derring-do. He floated beside it, holding on, figuring it out. He might only have one chance. If he tipped it, that could be that.

"Don't be stupid," he said to himself. "It's still going to float. You just won't be in it." He wanted to be in it, though. About as much as he had ever wanted anything.

From the troughs of the waves, all Ry could see was water and sky. And two mountaintops. No one would see him. From the crests he could see the port town. He could even make out a tiny flag, above a building. Given how hard it had been to reach the Zodiac, he doubted he could swim there.

The thing about trying to get into a dinghy when you are floating in bottomless depths is, there is nothing to push off from. It requires a lot of strength and energy which, depending on what you have just been doing, you might not have.

Trying to get into the dinghy with an inflated vest was, Ry decided, next to impossible. It was in the way, an inflated obstacle. Holding on with one hand, Ry worked his other hand down into the buttoned pocket of his shorts. He pulled out his pocketknife, felt with his teeth for the indentation in the blade to open it. He slashed the vest.

And then, in the same way the guy riding that camel with the goatskin full of milk invented cheese—which is to say, completely by accident—Ry discovered the best way to board an inflatable dinghy if you are floating next to it, which is that a swell comes up behind you and you sort of swim right in.

He sprawled, surprised and elated, adjusting to his new situation. He rode a couple of swells, just glad to be topside. The open pocketknife was still clenched in his fist. When he noticed how near it was to the inflated dinghy, he snapped it shut and carefully shifted to an upright position. From which he immediately saw how fast the *Peachy Pie* was going down. He didn't have much time: if he didn't cut the tow rope very, very soon, the dinghy would go down, too. Trying to stay balanced as the little boat was lifted by the swells and fell into the troughs, he leaned forward, gingerly, to grasp the rope and pull it toward him. Opening his knife once more, he hacked frantically at its sturdy fibers. It was not that great a knife.

He sawed away, not allowing himself to look up at the sinking sailboat. Halfway through, he peeked. Uh-oh. He sawed harder. He cut through the last stubborn strands. He tossed the rope away from him and watched it disappear.

And that's when the last beautiful bit of the *Peachy Pie* went under. That's when it occurred to him that the *Peachy Pie* was a beautiful expensive object that didn't belong to him, and he had just trashed it. He made a mental note to be sorry about that if and when he made it to shore. Really, really sorry. If and when.

Untethered, the wind blew him quickly away from the *Peachy Pie*. Though, how could you even tell?

His hands were trembling. Glancing down at them, he noticed that Yulia's phone number could still be read, though being in the water had washed some of it away. He knew her last name now, too. Unless Del had been hallucinating or something.

For a few minutes, Ry just sat, riding the waves. The wind entered his life jacket where he had slashed it. It billowed out from his chest, fluttering and flapping, reminding him how useless he had made it. He didn't need that. He took it off and pitched it.

He remembered that the Zodiac had a motor. He

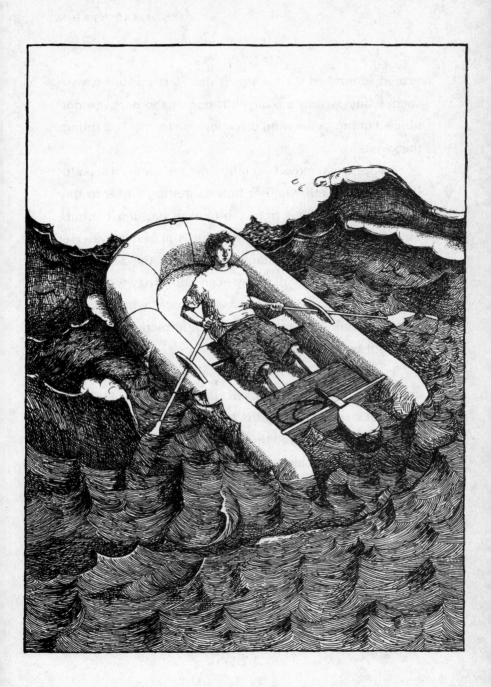

turned around to start it up. It did start up, but it was such a tiny farting motor. With one of the oars, he got himself going in the right direction. He focused on riding the swells.

Progress was slow. Glacially slow. Or maybe it wasn't. It was hard to tell whether he was getting closer to the island ahead, farther from the one he had left behind. The water just kept moving under him, sideways. He thought of the Polynesians, navigating the Pacific in dugout canoes. How did they even know they would get anywhere? And they didn't have motors. Maybe they had sails. He couldn't remember. He could picture sails, but he might be making that up.

Ry didn't know how much gas there was. He decided he'd better row, to help himself along. That meant he had to sit backward, turning his back on his goal. Also, he wouldn't be able to see the oncoming waves. He had to keep looking over his shoulder. Oh, well. So what?

It was discouraging, though, how he didn't seem to be getting anywhere. The oars seemed as useful as toothpicks. He started to keep his gaze just below St. Jeroen's for as long as he could, to stay on course without trying to measure his distance. He made himself sing songs, a whole song before he looked up. Traditional sea chanties—"Silent Night," "Happy Birthday," "The Alphabet Song," which could also be sung as "Twinkle Twinkle"—as well as some newer ones.

He started to make one up called, "I Hate the *#@! Ocean," but then, because it seemed like bad karma to insult Neptune at this time and place, he switched over to "The Ocean Is My Friend, My Beautiful, Beautiful Friend."

That's what Ry was singing, over and over, when the motor died. He tried a few times to start it again, but it was no use. The gas tank was empty. The dinghy had spun sideways. Facing Africa. All you had to do was cross the Atlantic. No sweat. Ry sat there, bobbing along. He looked to the right, toward Finisterre, staring without seeing. He was tired of keeping his spirits up. But no one else was going to do it. Were they.

Then his eyes came to the rescue. They could make out windows on the buildings, windows! He was getting there after all.

"Okay," he said. "Full Polynesian, now." He turned the boat. And he rowed. And rowed. And rowed. And rowed.

When he got close enough, the island and the sea relented and carried him in to shore on rolling, breaking waves. There was the final obstacle of dodging boulders and coral heads. If your only tool is a paddle, does everything look like water?

No. A rock is still a rock. Ry jabbed at it with his oar, trying to push away, and flipped himself over. He was under the surf. It moved him along and passed him by. Moved him farther and passed him by again; withdrew, sucking him backward. His hands and his toes scraped the bottom. Bracing himself against the pulling, pushing waves, he stood up. He was in waist-high water. On the average. He waited for the next wave and rode it in.

He crawled onto the warm sand. His stomach full of salt water, dehydrated, sunburned, physically spent, emotionally whipped, he passed out. The sun inched downward. The shadows grew longer. The rhythm of the waves was a lullaby.

# SEEING THINGS?

About thirty yards away, Ry's parents made ready to sail. Skip tested the bilge pumps. Wanda checked on the weather one more time. Once bitten, twice shy, and all that.

"Are we ready?" she asked.

"Almost," he said. "I just need ten, fifteen minutes."

"Hey," he said a moment later. "Do you think you could go grab us a couple of those saltfish-johnnycake sandwiches? I think I'm getting addicted to those things. And some bottles of water or juice or something."

"Okay," said Wanda. "Do you want anything else?"

"No," said Skip. "Just a sandwich and a drink. Here." He fished some bills and coins from his pocket and dumped them into her cupped hands.

"I think that's enough," he said. "Anyway, it's all we have left. Of cash."

Wanda counted the money up and put it in her own pocket. She walked one last time back into the little town, to the lunch cart in the square. She passed the fragrant and fishy grocery store, where the butter came in cans. From New Zealand. She passed the once elegant, now down on its luck hotel. Passing the small litter-strewn town beach, she almost cried out. A boy about Ry's age, he even had Ry's hair color, he was even *shaped* like Ry, lay sleeping on the beach, down near the water's edge. He slept like Ry, in the same position. She couldn't see his face. She felt an impulse to go tap the boy on the shoulder and make him look up at her.

"You're being ridiculous," she said to herself. "He'll think you're a nutcase." She didn't go over. She kept walking. It couldn't be, of course. Still, a pulling sensation passed through her.

As she was buying the sandwiches, she decided that on the way back, she would go over to the boy. She could say, "Oh, from the back, you look just like my son." That kind of thing happened all the time. Besides, who cared if he thought she was nuts? She would never see him again.

But when Wanda got there, the boy was gone. There was an impression in the sand. She spun around. He couldn't be far. She saw him, walking into Finisterre. He walked like Ry. She would go see; she just wanted to see this boy's face. Then she could let go of it.

Keeping her eyes on him, she half walked, half ran. Because she was watching him, trying to catch up, the voice at her elbow made her jump. She looked down. It was a goat. It was talking to another goat. When she looked up again, she could not find him in the lazy, busy square. She hurried over to where he had been. She turned around, scanning in every direction, willing him to appear.

After ten minutes she decided she was being foolish.

"You are on a tiny island," she said softly, "that no one has ever even heard of. How would your son be here?"

## IN FINISTERRE

Ry's rumbling stomach woke him. He raised himself onto his elbows, then to his hands and knees, and stood up. And blinked. The inside of his head was a solar oven, baking salty wet wads of tangled wool. He knew that time had passed, was passing now. He had to get moving. But he needed his brain, and that wasn't going to start up without some calories and some unsalted hydration.

As he walked into town, an isolated outpost of brain that was still functioning reported that there was a little money left in the sodden lump of wallet in his back pocket. It would be soggy, but probably was not yet pulp. Another outpost observed that the words on the cardboard sign hanging on the lunch cart were English words. Ry's head began to clear. The buildings that formed the edges of the square were two stories high, some of white and bright-colored wood and cement and some of very old-looking stone. Lots of porches on the second floor, with gingerbread woodwork on the railings and below the roof. Open porches, to catch the breeze. Shutters. Palm trees. Cars. People.

From where he stood, he could see two banks. He could change his wet American dollars into kopecks or drachmas or whatever kind of money people used here. He chose the bank that had "Canada" in its name and headed over. His shoes had become foot-torture devices, weighty saltwater-and-sand top-notch flesh abraders, but he was able to ignore them. He would take them off when he got out of the bank.

At first the woman behind the counter was not going to take Ry's wet money. She didn't have a place for wet money. She turned him down. He walked toward the door, temporarily defeated. Then he turned around and got in line again. She smiled when she saw him in front of her, but she turned him down again. He got in line again. This time her smile was wider. Like the door when you can get your foot in.

"I understand your situation," Ry said. "But I've been waving it around. Look, it's hardly even wet anymore.

"I'm from Wisconsin," he added. "Which is right next to Canada. We're, like, next-door neighbors."

"If you're my neighbor," she said, "how come I never saw you before?"

She took his damp bills, two tens, and gave him some Caribbean money. Ry thanked her and heaped blessings on her head and told her she had saved his life.

"Next, please," she said, looking past him. He hurried to the lunch cart in the square.

The lunch-cart woman was closing up shop, but Ry persuaded her to sell him most of what she had left at a reduced price. He sat down on the base of a clock tower in the middle of the square and took off his foul evil shoes. As he ate the first sandwich, he saw a familiar face.

"Hi," he called out, and waved.

"Hey," said the Austrylian. "Good sail?"

"It was awesome," said Ry. "You?"

"Amazing," said the Aussie. "Nothing like it."

"Where did you park your boat?" Ry asked.

"At the marina," said the A. He pronounced it "mareener."

"It's the only place you can, isn't it?"

"As far as I know," said Ry. "I thought you might know if there was anyplace else. You know, like the cove on St. Jeroen's."

"Not on this island," said the A. "Well, see you, then."

"See you," said Ry. "Back at the mareener."

Still eating, he walked in the direction of the water, his composting shoes tucked under one arm.

The Zodiac had washed up, and a handful of little kids were playing on it and around it.

"Hey," said Ry. They scattered, shrieking, and he laughed. He looked both ways. To the north, he could see masts poking up on the other side of a shrubbed spit of land. So he headed north.

It only took minutes to reach the marina. A couple of dozen boats were moored there. A few more were arriving; two were taking their leave. Ry eyed the departing boats with a flutter in his heart. One boat was huge—that would definitely not be them. The other one could be.

He walked around the harbor, looking. He didn't know what kind of boat he was looking for, or what it was called, only roughly what size it would be. He had to identify it by its occupants. Its crew. A lot of boats didn't have anyone on deck just now.

He didn't know what he would do if he didn't find them. In an odd way, he didn't even think about it, which surprised him. He knew he would do something. Maybe he was getting used to not knowing what happens next.

He saw a beautiful boat that reminded him of the *Peachy Pie*, and remembered to feel sorry, really sorry.

Wow. Yulia was not going to be happy. If he couldn't find his family, he could offer himself to her as an indentured servant to work off the cost. He looked at the faded number on his hand. He should have used a pen at the Canadian bank to reinforce it. Ry added memorizing the number to the mission of looking for his parents and their boat.

He said it aloud, over and over, as he walked.

Until a moving shape up ahead caught his eye. Ry stopped in his tracks. He smiled, laughed almost. It was really pretty brilliant what your brain, with the help maybe of your heart, could identify. All he saw, and from a fair distance, was a man's back. The man was only putting something into a trash can. Then the man stepped onto his boat. Ry could tell by the shape of the man, and how he moved, that this was his father.

And though he had made a mistake about that once as a child, he was certain that there was his father leaving, getting ready to sail away. His mother's immediately identifiable even in a life jacket mom-shape moved along the boat, checking in her mom way that all was in order. There was the boat, moving away from the dock. Ry was running now.

Holding them in his gaze, he didn't see the rope that had been left uncoiled in his path. He went flying through the air. The greasy bag of saltfish-johnnycake sandwiches flew from his clutch. The yellow shoes fell from under his arm. Boy, sandwiches, and shoes met weathered wood in that order, in varying degrees of injurious impact. Ry landed on his chin and his forearms. He was up in an instant. Running again, arriving at the place his parents had just left behind.

They were facing seaward, about four or five boat lengths out. Their tender trailed behind. Ry hurled himself into the water, a human torpedo. He rose to the surface, a human seal. He swam to the boat, a human . . . really good swimmer. A ladder climbed up the stern from the waterline. As Ry hauled himself up, a smile couldn't help forming. Peeking up over the transom, he saw his father studying the chart. His mother was sorting out the sheets and the halyards. He crawled onto the boat and came up behind her.

"Here, Mom," he said, "let me show you how that's done."

Teenage ninja cowboy sailing guy. Howdy, ma'am, can I help you with that halyard?

He hadn't counted on her fainting. Ry guessed he still had some things to learn. That was no surprise. He was an apprentice. It would take practice.

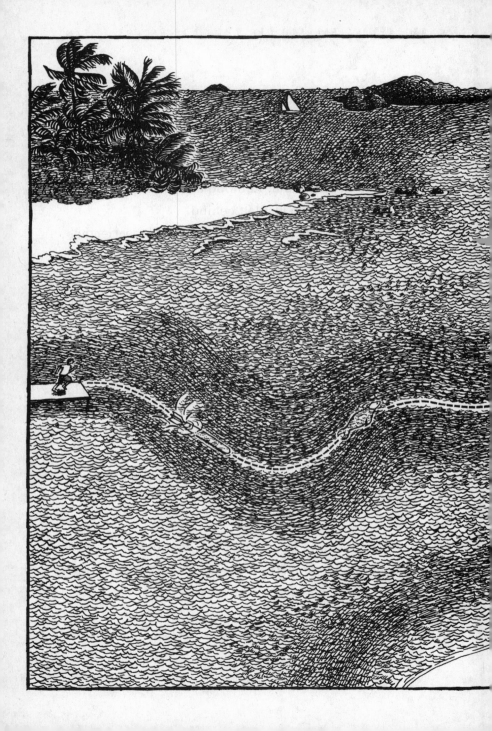

# DOGS

# THE NEWS

Back in Waupatoneka Betty and Lloyd settled in on the couch to watch the news. They had just returned from their trip—Betty's high school reunion, and a couple of days at her family's cabin on a lake in the woods. Lloyd's head was doing a lot better now. He knew who Betty was almost all the time, especially now that they had left her twin sister back in Illinois. And he liked her, even when he wasn't sure who she was. He liked her quite a bit. They watched the news holding hands.

Suddenly a fuzzy photograph of Lloyd appeared on the screen. An old one, taken at some birthday celebration. Now phrases popped up beside the photo, facts about Lloyd: his age, his height and weight, when he was last seen.

"Oh, dear," said Betty. "You're missing. I guess we better call that phone number. I'll go do it right now, before I forget."

She repeated the number to herself as she got up and went into the alcove in the hall. She was writing it down on the notepad there when the phone rang. She picked it up and squinted at it, searching for the Talk button.

"Hello?" she said. Then, "Yes?

"The dogs?

"Where?"

# DOGS

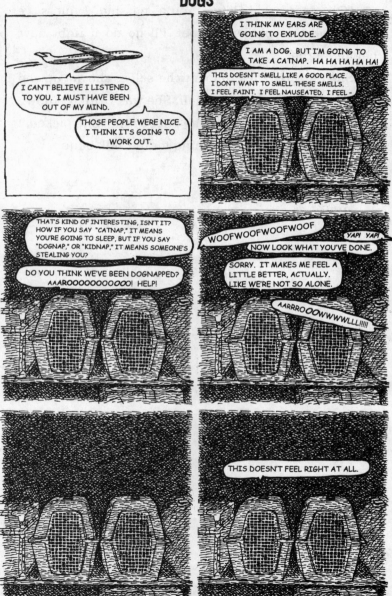

## SOME EXPLAINING TO DO

There was some explaining to do, to a variety of people: Parents. Authorities. Yulia.

Ry's parents wanted to see exactly what kind of nutcase he had gotten mixed up with.

"He's a really good kind of nutcase," said Ry.

"Tell me again why he's in this hospital?" asked his mother as they walked in. Ry didn't want to say that Del fell off a windmill. Not yet, anyway.

"He fell from a deck that had a rotten railing," he said.

When they entered the hospital room, Ry was so glad to see Yulia, he almost forgot that he had to tell her about the *Peachy Pie*. She rose from her chair to come give him a hug and to meet his mom and dad. She charmed them. Ry could feel the atmosphere lighten. Then she offered the only chair to Wanda and sat on

Del's bed, moving his plaster-encased legs right over.

Ry's father perched on the windowsill. Ry leaned against the wall. Everyone was being polite, but it couldn't help being an awkward occasion. Del asked Skip and Wanda about their vacation. Skip and Wanda didn't quite know what to ask Del, or Yulia.

Ry leaned against the wall, listening, helping things along where he could. It came to him as he leaned there that he didn't want to say good-bye to Del and Yulia. Not permanently. Then, too soon, the moment arrived for him to tell his part of the story. The part where he sank the boat.

"So Ry, how did you get to St. Jude's?" asked Yulia. "You didn't sail there alone, did you?"

Ry looked from her beautiful face to Del's. Despite being broken and glued back together like a china teapot, Del was happy.

"I was thinking," Ry said to him, "that it's going to take a while before you're really up and around. And by that time, I'll be in school. But maybe next summer we could build Yulia a new boat."

He hadn't been thinking that at all. It had entered his mind nanoseconds before it left his mouth. It appeared there like a miracle.

"It would be really educational for me," he said for

his parents' benefit, improvising, not knowing what he would say next. "And then you guys could come down and we could all go for a sail.

"Because the *Peachy Pie* is at the bottom of the ocean," he said, in a voice no one could have heard if the room had not become utterly quiet. His miracle idea seemed to die on the vine. It flickered in and out of existence.

One more idea came to Ry.

"Actually," he said, looking at Del, "I guess building a whole boat would be pretty much impossible." Having said the magic words, he mentally crossed his finger and looked away. He tried to appear downcast, pensive, resigned. It didn't require much acting.

He waited a beat.

Two beats.

Three.

Oh, well.

Then Del said, "I don't know about 'im*poss*ible.'"

# POSTSCRIPT

$Y$ou want to go off, have an adventure, be your own person. But first you want to make sure your family is all snugged in at home, not wandering loose like a bunch of stray cats. Or lost dogs. Otherwise, how do you call home for money? How do you get home in time for dinner, if no one's there cooking it up? Someone has to stay home.

Someone had stayed home. Then, one little thing went wrong—or, okay, a half dozen, a dozen, an unusually large number of things went wrong—and everyone went spinning off in all directions.

The interesting and amazing thing was that then they came back together. Invisible and visible forces, whatever you wanted to call them, could pull you back. Another interesting and amazing thing was, now there was Del and Yulia, and there was also Betty the Neighbor. Maybe the more people you put in your family, the better. Like a diversified investment portfolio.

Ry pulled on a clean T-shirt and went downstairs, gave the happy dogs a pat, and headed out the back door. He went for a spin on his bike, just checking out the old hometown. The new hometown.

The dead car junkyard was newly interesting. He wandered up and down, pushing his bike through the grass, looking over the rows of defunct vehicles. No Willyses. Some awesome ones, though.

He rode on and came to a park. A bike path threaded through it, alongside a small lake. Lake Waupatoneka. The path went over a low bridge across a creek that ran into the lake. On impulse, Ry parked his bike and hopped up onto the concrete railing. He walked across. He walked back and jumped down and got back on his bike.

On the far side of the park, the path continued, following the edge of the lake. Sometimes there was a sliver of beach between the path and the lake, sometimes not. A few sailboats scudded along. It was blowing. There were motorboats and Jet Skis, too. The sound of voices and the fragrance of grilling and barbecue floated through the air. Ry came up behind a girl around his age who was wading along, hauling a Sunfish behind her by the rope. The sail was down, dragging a little in the water, the mast was rattling in its pocket, the rudder clunked, and the whole thing rollicked up and down over the wake of a passing motorboat. It looked like a slog. Ry slowed down unintentionally, out of curiosity, to match her pace. She noticed, scowled slightly, and kept going. She was beautiful in this interesting, stubborn, scowling, drowned-rat kind of way. She had clearly gone under a few times.

Ry had stopped. Now he pedaled to catch up and called out, "Why don't you just sail it?"

"Too much wind," she answered. Retorted, you could say. "It's impossible."

Ry watched as she slogged on. Then he caught up to her again, got slightly ahead, laid down his bike, kicked off his shoes, and came down to the water's edge.

"I don't know about 'im*poss*ible," he said.

# POST-POSTSCRIPT: PEG AND OLIE

# EXTRAS

## AS EASY AS FALLING
### OFF THE FACE OF THE
# EARTH

Lynne Rae Perkins talks about the making of
*As Easy as Falling Off the Face of the Earth*
and shares Peg and Olie's story.

# A Book
## You Should Read

Several years ago, I read a book called *The Laughing Sutra*, by Mark Salzman. I really liked it. It's sort of a retelling of a very old fable, but set in modern times, in China and in California. It's an adventure story with fantastic elements; it's smart and funny and moving. I gave it to my son, who was thirteen at the time, and then to some of his friends. He liked it; they liked it, too.

In a review I read, *The Laughing Sutra* was described as "picaresque." I wasn't exactly sure what that meant, so I looked it up. It seems to be a type of story told in episodes, usually about the adventures of a rogue or antihero living by his wits on the road. One of the earliest and most famous picaresque novels was *Don Quixote*, by Miguel de Cervantes. So I read that, as well as *Lazarillo de Tormes*, which was published anonymously but is probably by Diego Hurtado de Mendoza—apparently it is one of the first picaresque tales ever. I decided I wanted to write one, too . . . which led to this book, *As Easy as Falling Off the Face of the Earth*.

All this is to say I think you should read *The Laughing Sutra*, by Mark Salzman. I think you'll like it.

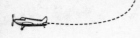

# Drawings
# I Didn't
# Draw

Words and pictures, pictures and words. One or the other, or both? Here are some of the things I thought about drawing but decided to leave to the reader's imagination:

The lumpy, grassy hills of eastern Montana. The ArchaeoTrails camp logo. The little animal skull. The double-decker truck. The Think Twice Tree Service logo. Pete. Pete's tattoos. Arvin's eyes. The monkey in the banyan roots, with the cell phone. Dream fragments: stairs, chasms, etc. The lifeless speedometer with dead bugs in it. Carl's car on two wheels. Lloyd and Betty, Ry and Del, passing in opposite directions on the highway. Roads twisting like spaghetti. The funky shadow of a staircase on a huge cylindrical tank. The level of mosquito saturation in the Florida night. Everett's methane digester exploding. The tiny plane over the Caribbean. Lulu and Ry in the back of the plane. The landing strip. The cat in its tutu/cat door. Del walking on Yulia's roof. Ry's face, Naruto-style. The birthday-cake-with-candle island. Map/diagram: *la ultima isla*. A goat's eyes: the pupils are horizontal slits. The "Dutch" miller with dreadlocks. Ry in his life jacket, floating like a lily pad with his legs dangling. Ry's mom seeing him sleeping on the beach.

# Preamble
## for Dog Audio
## Script

$W$hile I was working on this book, I had a plot diagram pinned to the wall beside my desk that looked like this:

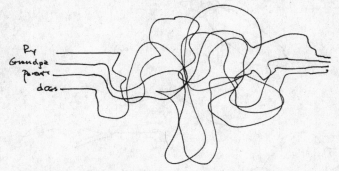

Ry's story was the most important, but I wanted everyone to wander off and have an adventure, an odyssey, a story of their own.

One day in the studio, the idea popped into my head that it would be funny if the dogs went on an *Incredible Journey*-type adventure, but that Olie, the one who was the brave and fearless leader, would also be clueless and lead them completely astray. Somehow, by pure luck, they would wind up at their home, and Olie would be convinced that he had succeeded.

A string of brief conversations between the two dogs popped into my head (who knows how these things happen) and I scribbled them down, along with some scribbly little dog sketches. It seemed to me that their story should be mostly told in pictures. It seemed more doggy. Although they were having conversations. With words. But the conversations were really more like subtitles for a movie in a foreign language, if the person who wrote the subtitles (me) doesn't actually know the foreign language (dog), but maybe took two years of it in high school (have a dog, but am not personally one myself).

So, pictures.

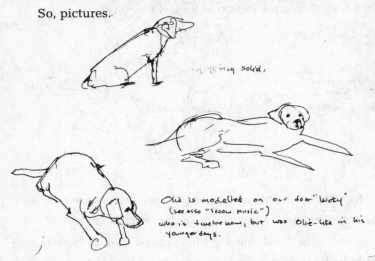

*getting solid,*

*Olie is modelled on our dog "Woky" (see also "Snow Music") who is twelve now, but was Olie-like in his younger days.*

And then the audio book of *As Easy as Falling Off the Face of the Earth* came along. No pictures. What to do—should we just leave the dogs' story out? No, not that!

So I wrote out a script. It was fun. It almost wrote itself, which doesn't happen for me very often.

Keep in mind as you read the segments that they pop up sporadically between the other parts of the story. So sometimes they refer to the other stories. And remember, it's an audio script. Maybe you should read it aloud. With drama.

# Dog
# Audio

*These first three little segments should be read immediately after "A FARAWAY BUT RELATED STORY: WISCONSIN" (p. 85) and immediately before "ANOTHER FARAWAY BUT RELATED STORY, THIS ONE WITH A BEAUTIFUL SUNSET" (p. 88).*

## A FARAWAY BUT RELATED STORY: DOG VERSION

Olie, the black dog, noticed that the man kept falling down. He was down now. He seemed to be asleep, only different than that somehow.

Peg, the red dog, decided the man needed help. She decided that she would go get some and that Olie should stay with the sleeping man.

Olie watched her go. He wanted to go, too. With Peg. Why should just Peg get to go?

He could go.

He *would* go.

He went.

As he headed down the path after Peg, someone was coming from the other direction. A person. Toward the man who had fallen down.

On her way to get help, Peg came upon an excellent-smelling bit of nature.

Mmmm. . . . *Wow.* She rolled over and rubbed her back fur

into it for maximum pleasure. And forgot for a moment where she was, what she was doing.

Then she remembered and moved on, but the dratted leash got caught in the fork of a scrubby tree. She pulled, trying to yank herself free, but she was stuck.

Now Olie, coming after her, came upon the good smell. He, too, participated in it. As he lay on his tummy, regrouping, he heard a familiar "Woof."

It was Peg.

Something was wrong.

Peg was glad to see Olie. Glad for once that he hadn't followed directions. He chewed the leash until she was free, and together they raced to the house. But it wasn't right; the house felt empty. It was Olie who remembered that the guy was in the woods. *Duh.* But when they came back out of the garage, there was the guy, getting into a car. *What?*

They ran, but this time it was Olie's leash that got stuck, in a curly ornamental flowerbed fence thing. By the time he got free, the guy was gone.

Now what?

The two dogs waited on the porch.

He would come back.

■ ■ ■

*This next one comes immediately after "ANOTHER RELATED BUT FARAWAY STORY, THIS ONE WITH A BEAUTIFUL SUNSET," (p. 90) and immediately before "AT THE END OF THE DAY" (p. 92).*

# DOG

The two dogs waited on the porch.

They waited. And waited.

Olie remembered that movie about the two dogs and the cat who find their way home, even though they have to travel hundreds—maybe it was even thousands—of miles to get there. Really far. They can find their way because they have "instinct."

Maybe that was what had happened to them. Maybe they needed to find their way back to *their* old house.

They waited. They waited in different positions: sitting up, lying down, sitting up again.

The guy didn't come back.

Still. The day changed colors.

They would have to do it, the finding-their-way thing. Peg sighed.

The two dogs, the red one and the black one, moved down the road toward the sunset, dragging their long shadows behind them.

■ ■ ■

*This one should come immediately after the art spread that follows "NORTH DAKOTA" (pp. 132–33) and immediately before "ROAD TALK" (p. 136):*

# DOGS

Side by side, Peg and Olie headed for home. Their old home. Wherever it was. They would find it, because they were dogs. With instinct.

An opportunity arose to climb down from a retaining wall into the back of a pickup truck, and instinct said, Do it. They rode. Their ears flapped in the breeze. They were road dogs.

When the truck stopped again, they jumped out, just for a minute, but then there was no wall, no way to climb back in. The truck left without them.

Oh. Well.

They picked their paws up and put them down.

Picked 'em up and put 'em down.

■ ■ ■

*This next bit should be inserted in the chapter "ROAD TALK" after the sentence, "I mean, it wasn't life threatening," (end of p. 141) and before the sentence "Everything was still, except for the light, peaceful snoring" (top of p. 142).*

The dogs, Peg and Olie, were on a part of their journey that was far from anywhere, and they were so tired. Dog tired. It was dark, but the earth was still warm. They curled up together somewhere in warm grass that smelled like the very long sunny day. They snoozed. They had dreams, too. Hunting dreams, running dreams. Full-food-bowl dreams. In Peg's dream, she couldn't find her food bowl. Her stomach growled. But it didn't wake her up.

At first light, in the Willys, Del did not wake up, but Ry did. *(We rejoin the regular text. Notice that "At first light, in the Willys," etc., is a new bit of transitional text to separate the dog bit from the next bit.)*

■ ■ ■

*This next bit is after the chapter "ROAD TALK" (p. 147) and before the chapter "KIND OF WEIRD" (p. 149):*

## DOGS

The dogs were eating out, too. They licked at the remains of meals in Styrofoam take-out containers. Gulped stray French fries and lapped up melted milkshakes.

Peg killed a bird. She didn't even plan to, she had never done it before, she just did it, and there it was. It was feathery, and full of little bones.

Eating out can seem fun and glamorous, when you are eating the same chow, every day. You wouldn't think you could get tired of it. But you can. It doesn't take long.

■ ■ ■

*After "YOU ARE HERE" (p. 206) and before "TENNESSEE. GEORGIA.
FLORIDA." (p. 209):*

## DOGS

One way of putting what was happening with Olie and Peg
might be to say they were lost. Peg was leaning toward that
theory. Nothing looked right. Nothing smelled familiar. And it
was taking a long, long time.

Olie was an optimist. They had probably been sleeping in
the car when the family drove through this part. And riding in
the car was faster than walking. Or at least it seemed faster,
because you could sleep.

Those mountains, though, those snow-capped mountains.
Neither of them had ever seen anything like that before. Those
mountains were something to wonder about.

What the heck, thought Olie. But he kept that thought to
himself. He kept his ears cocked, all sprightly. He didn't let on.

■ ■ ■

*The next bits come after "In Finisterre" (p. 341) and before "THE
NEWS" (p. 344) and then after "The News" (p. 345) and before "SOME
EXPLAINING TO DO" (p. 345):*

## DOGS

Olie and Peg huddled together in a city, in a doorway next
to a sidewalk, behind curtains of raindrops. They were cold,
wet, and hungry. And muddy. They were lost. And, though they

were glad to have each other, they were lonely. For people. For a house. People whizzed past in cars, but no one stopped. No one opened a door and said, "Go for a ride?"

But here was someone, someone bending over and speaking soft words, looking at their jingle-tags. Olie wagged his tail. He couldn't help it. He was easy.

"Holy-moly!" the person said. "How did you end up here?"

Olie licked the person's face.

The house was nice. The people were nice. The food was nice. But just when they were getting used to being there, Olie and Peg were gently coaxed into plastic boxes. They could see out through slots and a wire door, but they couldn't get out. There was a car ride in the boxes. Then jostling, shouting, and loud, loud noises. Peg felt faint, nauseated. Her ears were popping.

Olie felt chipper. He cracked dog jokes.

Peg howled.

Other dogs, apparently also trapped in this loud dark vibrating scary place, howled with her. That made her feel better.

But not much.

■ ■ ■

*This next bit is at the very, very, very end.*

## POST–POSTSCRIPT: PEG AND OLIE

Peg and Olie were home again, in the new house, with their people and their food dishes and giant-sized rawhide "bones." How did it happen? Maybe, Peg thought, Olie was smarter than she ever gave him credit for.

Just then, one of Olie's toenails got hooked in a link of the chain at the front of his collar as he maneuvered for a better angle on his rawhide. He struggled to release it. But he only had to struggle briefly. The mother walked through the room, saw Olie's predicament, and figured it out. She fixed it, chirping and murmuring, then went on her way. Olie continued chewing, unperturbed.

Or maybe, Peg thought, he was just lucky.